About the authors

Marcelo Coutts and Stuart Godwin are advertising creative directors whose work has graced the airwaves and surfaces in multiple countries across the world and collected many advertising awards along the way. Writing books seemed like a logical extension to their collaboration. *Napoleon and the Cook with No Name* is their second book together. Their first book, *Goya's Secret,* was released in 2024.

Marcelo Coutts

Marcelo Coutinho, aka Marcelo Coutts, was born in 1969 in Ourinhos, State of São Paulo, Brazil. He studied communication and design at São Paulo State University (UNESP). A veteran advertising man, Marcelo worked as a creative director at agencies such as Grey, D'Arcy, Leo Burnett, McCann and Havas in Europe, where his creativity collected many advertising awards.

Stuart Godwin

Stuart Godwin was born in South Africa in 1967. He holds a postgraduate degree in English literature from Johannesburg University. He's been a demolitions squad leader, a cook, a lecturer, a divemaster, a journalist, a usability evangelist, a business analyst, a brand consultant, and an advertising creative director, the latter role taking him around the world.

Napoleon and the Cook with No Name

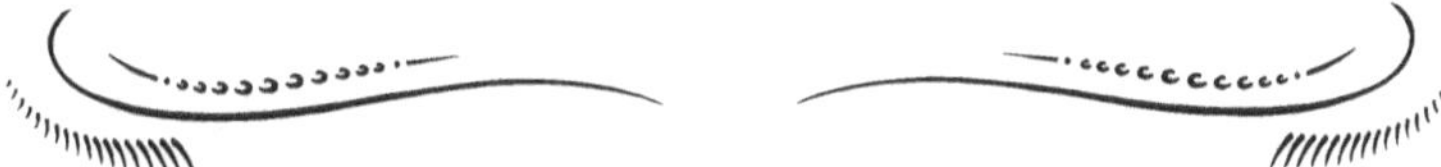

Marcelo Coutts and Stuart Godwin

Napoleon and the Cook with No Name

Pegasus

PEGASUS PAPERBACK

A CIP catalogue record for this title is
available from the British Library

ISBN-978-1-80468-063-6

Pegasus is an imprint of
Pegasus Elliot MacKenzie Publishers Ltd.
www.pegasuspublishers.com

First Published in 2025

Pegasus
Sheraton House Castle Park
Cambridge CB3 0AX England

Printed & Bound in Great Britain

Dedication

I dedicate this book to my wife, Letícia, who is the light that illuminates my path. Her love and infinite patience guided me through the sleepless nights I spent creating this book. I also dedicate this book to my friend Stuart, who had the patience to translate, organise and structure the story of *Goya's Secret* and *Napoleon and the Cook with No Name.*

Marcelo Coutts

I dedicate this book first and foremost to my buddy, Marcelo, who is the most creative person I have ever met, and without whom this book would simply not exist. I also dedicate this book to Petra, who puts up with my grumpiness and is a constant source of cheer.

Stuart Godwin

Acknowledgements

This book relies on numerous contributions, and we would like to express our gratitude to everyone at the museums and libraries who inspired us.

We give special thanks to Giuseppe Pandolfo, known as 'Pino', from Sant'Arsenio, for his guidance on various Italian facts. 'Prego'!

Preface

Marcelo and Stuart are writers and artists, and they wrote this book as a great gift for readers. Their writing births a new, ageless literature style, entertaining while beckoning your heart to discover more and more about the philosophic story between the real and unreal world.

The illustrations are truly pieces of art, only adding to the reader's imagination as they traverse the universe of this book. Ambition, war, power, and selfishness are strong elements of most characters, but by creatively weaving in elements of dreams and magic, the authors touch you with a sense of peace, wisdom, and fantasy.

The cook with no name is a smart, self-educated character who, through his own special gastronomy, wishes the food he prepares can control a person's inner equilibrium, the very body, mind, and soul that can bring about peace and kindness.

This fantastic work reminds you that power and money wither away when you die, but peace and love live on forever.

Above all, the story in Napoleon and The Cook With No Name is a grand life lesson, teaching that by being authentically you, your - 'no named' - self, one day after another, you can conquer your divine kingdom and achieve your own personal life victory.

Dircene DI'Angelo A.M.Martins

Artist, Instructor HCC Houston, TX - USA

Looking west from St. Helena.

CHAPTER 1

The big man at the top of the stairs

"Kings are the slaves of history."

Leo Tolstoy, War and Peace

The sound of ten-thousand thundering hooves beating across the Camargue in Louis Marchand's dream gives way to the reality of some belligerent and unknown force pounding on his bedroom door. Four o' clock in the morning. *Merde*, he thinks, as he tries to unglue eyes sticky with sleep. Unhappily, and half-awake, he accepts the miserable fact that he's not in France, atop a galloping white horse foaming at the bit. No, he's still in this godforsaken place, on this godforsaken rock, at the end of the earth, beyond the gates of the sun.

Somehow, he manages to stumble out of bed without hurting himself and wipes a nose, runny with snot, on the least crusty arm of his nightgown. If only it weren't for this infernal, eternal damp. Hades itself must have reached its sticky breath upwards to consume the very souls who inhabited this miserable, black-rat-infested dwelling they called Longwood House.

Damn it! I'm coming. As if it weren't punishment enough to be confined to this mouldy place, now it seemed a man was not even allowed to get a good night's sleep.

He coughs several times, a rattling bark that summons a goodly glob of phlegm. It's been like this since he arrived here in December 1815 – phlegm, damp, snot, and misery.

On his way to the door, he stops at a mahogany washstand to douse his face. He dips his hands into the exquisite blue and white patterned crockery basin and splashes the cold water onto the visibly shocked visage that stares back at him from the little mirror perched above the bowl.

The basin has a more interesting and storied history than most people on the island, its having reputedly been a gift from a Chinese Emperor to the Empress Josephine, who in turn was in the habit of giving away gifts that she didn't like to servants or anyone else who came into her presence. Louis must have had the unfortunate turn of luck to have been passing in front of the woman on just such an occasion. Or perhaps fortunate is a better word, because aside from its aesthetic charm, the basin is a finely crafted and functional piece of furniture that's more than quite serviceable and certainly fit for purpose. And to good purpose it certainly had been put, since it has removed the need for Louis to make the perilous journey to and from the bathrooms in this building whose walls are as diabolically cold as the icy rocks that surround them. It's so cold that the coldness seemed to creep into your bones and freeze them from the inside out.

Finally, he reaches the heavy door and struggles with the key. The latch and the lock mechanism have long ago rusted themselves into a state of non-cooperation – sea air and lack of maintenance have found their way into everything, including the souls of those who inhabit the big house. This beautiful, depressing shithole in the middle of an unforgiving ocean is as rusty as the souls of those who put me here, he thinks, rusty and corroded as the Big Man upstairs. *Merde,* even my bones are rusty.

The door creaks open with the sound of an old wooden ship adrift in a storm. There stands a redcoat. Louis fixes him with a malevolent stare and berates him with a few choice words in French. What in the name of all that is holy is the meaning of this intrusion? This is certainly not an appropriate time to be banging on people's doors. Did he not know that a man's resting hours were sacred?

The soldier, a snappy young Englishman whose French is as clearly rusty as everything else, takes a half step back, and does his best to maintain his composure. He returns Louis' gaze with an equally steely look and declares, in English, that no-one is interested in Louis' protestations, and that he, Louis, assistant to the Big Man upstairs, should stand to, and look lively in doing so. He wants to see you, immediately.

Louis hastily pulls on his clothes, which, although of the good variety, now sport several patches sewn onto the garment in the weak light of candles or Nordic fish-oil lamps. The result is a patchwork that looks in places like Nordic fishing boat sails that have been stitched by Vikings on their way to Valhalla.

* * *

The Big Man upstairs was, of course, not a reference to God, but rather to the person who lived on the top floor. And to whom everyone, including his British guards, had once paid a certain deference.

Things had been very different before the arrival of the new Governor some ten years ago. Despite being technically confined, the occupant of the top floor had nonetheless been treated well by his previous wards, who had made every effort to keep him happy.

He had been allowed to run this little empire here on the windswept plains of St. Helena like his own private court away from court. He wrote memoirs, issued orders, and was even allowed to explore the island on horseback, a luxury that, in retrospect, could not be underestimated, given the current state of things.

But the English, in their wisdom, had seen fit to despatch a new jailer in the personage of one Sir Hudson Lowe, an overly officious administrator, who had come into immediate conflict with the island's sole detainee, and who had apparently made it his sole mission to make life as miserable for the prisoner as he possibly could. To this end, Governor Lowe did more than just insult his prisoner's dignity. He curtailed the man's freedom of movement and made him present himself personally each morning under the pretext that he might escape.

Feeling mishandled and insulted, the prisoner, and one-time ruler of all Europe, withdrew from sight, boarding himself up inside Longwood and refusing to interact with the

Governor at all. He even spread rumours about absurd escape plots designed to irritate Lowe, such as building a wooden submarine, a feat that even if it were remotely conceivable, would never have survived the cordon of British gunships that surrounded St. Helena. Slowly and somewhat sulkily, however, the Big Man had had to come to terms with the fact that this was not going to the same as Elba. And to make things even more miserable, his health had begun to deteriorate some years back with his condition becoming increasingly worse of late. Marchand suspected Lowe had been slowly poisoning the once great emperor to silence him conclusively.

But it was now the end of January 1821. And whatever anybody thought the British might have been up to, they had so far failed to achieve it.

*

* *

Climbing the cold stairs to the room at the top, Louis passes the new physician who replaced the original doctor, Barry O'Meara. Although the new man did his best, he couldn't possibly hope to fill the shoes – or indeed that new-fangled device, the stethoscope – of O'Meara. And how could he? O'Meara had been with the Big Man since La Rochelle, had even volunteered to accompany him on the journey to this god-forsaken rock. No indeed, O'Meara had become a great deal more than a mere physician tending to the needs of his patient. He had been a companion and confident, spending considerable hours in the company of his friend, pursuing various amusements and discussions on such important topics as warfare, military strategy, and women. O'Meara had once confided in Marchand that he was keeping a journal, at the Big Man's suggestion, and had even allowed him a peak at the pages. Such was the rapport between the doctor and his charge.

As time went on however, the doctor saw his role grow into that of a buffer, protecting his patient from the cantankerous and pernicious influence of Governor Lowe. This so infuriated Lowe, who saw the two of them as being somehow in cahoots, that he mounted a relentless campaign of pressure to have O'Meara removed from the island. He succeeded. O'Meara was unceremoniously deported back to England.

The replacement physician was a dour, sarcastic creature, who went about with a lowered head and always seemed to be hiding something. Marchand had had a run-in with him when he had first arrived. In the ensuing argument the new man had said something along the lines of "…there are many ways to lose one's head. Pray that doing so in an argument should be enough for you." It was a clear threat; an allusion to the evil guillotine of Dr Joseph-Ignace. May his head be removed a thousand times by his own infernal device.

The Big Man's door is open, and Louis has no time to compose himself before entering. The room is a pandemonium of papers and notes strewn everywhere. A maid had once tried to tame the disorder, only to be turfed violently out with the bellowed exhortation, "…where you see mess, I see the means to confront the very soul of Julius Caesar!"

Indeed, now, here among the disarray, Louis spots several pressings dealing with Cesar and other things Roman. It was understood that the great Roman emperor was a favourite of this great French emperor. Perhaps the great Roman would have reciprocated the admiration.

Louis comes face to face with his commander, thinking in that moment how wrong the world is in their characterisation of him. The Petit Corporal is anything but petit.

Forgoing the niceties that would have softened the insanity of the hour, Napoleon Bonaparte speaks a single, emphatic sentence to his assistant:

Louis, I need you to get out of here and find him. Bring me the cook with no name.

Old Luc. Long in the tooth, big on heart.

CHAPTER 2

Tuberosum

"It's time to plant potatoes. We need a little digging in our lives."
Coutts and Godwin

Some three-and-a-bit decades prior to this conflab between the one-time Emperor-of-all-he-surveyed and his humble but loyal personal valet and servant, Louis Marchand, another story, no less important to our version of history, is taking place in some unnamed banlieue on the outskirts of Paris.

It's a miserable time for anyone not born into a noble caste. But looking back from our perspective, the year 1787 was no more or less special than its predecessors, being simply one among a succession of difficult years; it was merely the relentless unspooling of history towards an event that would forever change the course of Europe.

Many had no choice other than to live off the land. But planting and harvesting were gruelling and strenuous tasks, even for those who chose the relatively new and reliable potato plant. The climate at the time was uncharacteristically cold, causing the soil to freeze and the farmer's hands to bleed from the effort of turning it over.

Jean Pierre Lacroix was undoubtedly luckier – and savvier – than most. He'd managed to buy the smallholding of land that he counted as his own with the gold and jewels he'd earned in a previous life. He was not proud of his past, but that's a story for another day. What is germane at this juncture is that Jean Pierre was, for all intents and purposes, a farmer of potatoes.

Why it was that he chose potatoes may never be known. What is known is that he succeeded in growing them even where others struggled, consistently making a profit from year to year. Where others fell afoul of winters that took too long to ease into spring, Jean Pierre seemed to have a sixth sense about calculating the optimal dates for planting. Where many complained of an uncertain year ahead, Jean Pierre applied himself to the discovery of unique and better horticultural solutions.

Another source of considerable grievance for farmers at that moment in history was the seigneurial system. The seigneurial system was in many respects a French version of feudalism, but with one important distinction – it was largely an economic construct and had none of the reciprocal protections of feudalism. It forced ordinary people who worked and lived of the land to make significant remittances to the lords who owned not only that land, but also most of the modes of production.

Some farmers tried to arrange themselves into cooperatives, thinking that by combining land they might create an advantage. Bartering, too, was seen as a way to get around the absurd taxes levied by the corrupt noblemen. But this was nevertheless a difficult living, and many simply could not survive in this manner.

A man of no small ingenuity, Jean Pierre always found a way around these disadvantages. Despite his rustic demeanour, he was a naturally creative man who managed to hatch a scheme to profit from his endeavours.

He had a very simple plan to attract more customers and keep them loyal to him. His secret idea was as cunning as it was simple – to wash his potatoes in the stream near the plantation to remove the dirt. You can well imagine how those clean tubers must have appeared, sitting alongside those of his competitors, which were still covered in mud, insects, horse dung and whatever else nature, in all her wisdom saw fit to visit upon them.

Very soon, because of his resourcefulness, he was able to bypass the fray and confusion of the local markets, delivering his crop directly to the restaurants and mansions of the nobles in Paris. Here his customers valued – and more importantly, were able to pay for – what they perceived as a higher quality product. And this translated comfortably into lot more money for only a little more work.

There were still those who looked down upon the lowly grower, people who, for their own reasons, believed that a man who worked in the fields and smelled of pig shit was worthy only of their contempt. But there were others who gave compliments and marvelled how a man so brutish in appearance and trade could be so well mannered and spoken. They wondered whether he was an educated man, of whom a hard life had made a farmer.

Whatever the circumstances that had put him here, Jean Pierre was content. Little by little, he felt his lot in life improving. The extra money came in handy at a time when money was scarce. On top of this, it had been a good harvesting season and he had been able to save a small profit to see him through the approaching winter.

Until the letter arrived.

It was a bolt from the blue.

The missive was from the only woman who had ever managed to capture his heart. Laetitia Borriana Francisconi. She was ill. She needed him. And this was all that mattered.

*

* *

And so, on an October morning in 1787, we find Jean Pierre Lacroix moving to and from the stables on his smallholding, carrying camping equipment, blankets, and provisions for a long journey, wondering why his useless stable hand is drunk yet again. The sight of the man skulking uselessly about does nothing to alleviate his already black mood. He aims a boot at the ne'er-do-well's bony backside and watches him scamper away like the miserable soul that he is. Jean Pierre curses himself for having had to put up with the man this long, and resolves to sack him the next time he sees him. For now, that will have to wait.

He walks to the far end of the row of stalls where his trusty steed, Luc, hears his approach, and whinnies his own horsey hello. Despite being rather long in the tooth and exhibiting the pronounced separation of the ribs that suggests an age of around twenty-one years, the horse looks well cared for. He's too old to be ridden, but is still more than capable of pulling the light cart that Jean Pierre has stowed his equipment in.

He greets Luc with a bon jour and a carrot, which the horse snatches happily and eagerly with narrow, yellowed teeth. Jean Pierre lets Luc out of the stall to munch on a bale of hay as he hitches his small cart to the beast.

The cart itself appears to be of a similar vintage as the horse, and has been cobbled together from a collection of mismatched wheels, panels and other pieces salvaged from several predecessors that are now lying in pieces, either completely covered with grass and purple sweet pea vines, or home to families of small rodents and various poultry.

With his own rump ensconced on a blanket on the jump seat, Jean Pierre flicks Luc's hindquarters lightly with a leather switch, and sets off amidst the creaking of wheels that cry a song of friction and the scraping of wood on metal. Not even whale blubber can appease the heart of this archaic conveyance that Jean calls a cart. Both he and Luc are used to the sound of the complaining machine, however, and know from experience that the noise will abate once the wood starts to warm up and settle into the task at hand.

A few meters past the gate post, Jean Pierre stops, jumps from the cart and rushes back to the house. He reappears moments later, grumbling under his breath at having forgotten something important. In one hand he holds two leather bags – one containing coin, and the other, ammunition. In the other hand he carries his two weapons wrapped in an oil-cloth – a flintlock carbine, and an old, long-barrelled arquebus, whose origin he cannot remember.

He stows everything carefully in the cart and grabs the reigns once again. In the confusion of his anger at the stable hand and his own absent-mindedness of setting off without any means of defence, he's almost forgotten the sad purpose of his journey.

A tear slides down the scarred cheek of this rugged man's face. The unrequited love of his life is dying. He still loves her very much, even though fate has decreed that she can never be by his side.

Jean Pierre sets off.

CHAPTER 3

Flintlock

"The mechanical sciences are the noblest and most useful of all, because through them all animate bodies perform the operation for which they were designed."
Leonardo DaVinci

Several days into the journey, the old cart is creaking happily along on its equally old bearings. Curiously, the bearings are the only part of the cart that hadn't once been part of something else. Jean Pierre smiles as a thought pops into his head – the bearings were manufactured by the family of an old friend in Italy and came with an amusing story of their own. One side swore that they had been manufactured after the design first proposed by Leonardo da Vinci in the 15th century. The other side postulated that it was not Il Florentine who was responsible for inventing bearings, but rather, the Romans, during the time of Caligula, some fourteen-hundred years earlier. Either way, their song remains the same.

Amid these happy reminiscences on the part of his master, Luc suddenly whinnies and bucks his head in defiance of the bit. Jean Pierre feels a chill run up his spine. Old Luc has a nose for trouble and can usually sniff it out long before his master can. Jean has seen this same ability in his grandfather's donkey, although in the case of the mule, the animal would stop short, one leg in air, stubbornly refusing to go any further. Luc, on the other hand, has apparently not developed the good sense to stop, and presses on.

Jean Pierre squints into the distance. About a quarter of a mile distant, the road curves to pass through a small thicket of trees, casting it into comparatively dark shadow. As he gets closer, he spies a movement behind a gnarled trunk, as two men spring out. He's seen this trick before. Their ragged clothes and aggressive demeanour announce exactly who and what they are. Bandits. Highway robbers. Not uncommon in these parts, despite the penalty being a rather final visit to the gallows.

In the blink of an eye, Jean Pierre has the already-loaded-and-prepared flintlock out of its cover and aimed at the nearest-most bandit. The gun is a particularly fine specimen of the breech-loading variety, manufactured on the La Chaumette system. Its tapering barrel is finished in fire-blued metal, with flat-running sights extending almost the length of the barrel and brass foresight. This is complemented by an intricately decorated loading aperture, iron quick-threaded breech plugs with brass sleeve and blued tang. All mated with a classic walnut stock with finely engraved and chiselled ornamentation from the pattern book De Lacollombe.

It's as deadly as it is beautiful. And now it spits fire and hot lead.

As the puff of blue smoke dissipates, Jean Pierre can see the result of his marksmanship. The ball has struck his attacker above the bridge of the nose, creating a perfectly symmetrical third eye. If he'd measured and marked the shot with a measuring stick, he couldn't have gotten more precise. He's not proud of his proficiency with the weapon, nor is he excited by what he has just done. This is an awful echo of the man he was in a distant past. A past that he has worked hard to leave behind.

The dead man's accomplice and brother, a Swiss pirate named Jean-Francois DuClerc, gawps in horror at the half kneeling, crumpled body. The now defunct man's two natural eyes have rolled up inside his shattered skull, and blood is weeping out of the third like a horrible stigma from a crucifixion that never happened.

The old the bandit leaps into the undergrowth like a startled lynx. Despite the weight of his heavy pirate pistol, the speed of his escape seems to defy the laws of physics.

Jean Pierre alights from his cart and looks at the pathetic body that was once a scourge on these sylvan surroundings. He makes the sign of the cross and briefly contemplates trying to bury the man. No, this will take up valuable time, and his mission comes first. Besides, the other bandit might return with reinforcements, and he might not be as lucky next time.

*

* *

The journey continues without further mishap. His goal is to skirt the town of Chambéry and then head towards Valloire, quietly passing between the pre-alpine splendour of the Chartreuse and Bauges Mountains, and thence onwards to the northwest corner of the kingdoms of Italy.

After a time, he arrives in the territory of an old comrade, coincidently, also a Pierre; Francois Pierre. Here he will rest and take in fresh food and water. Old Luc, too, he knows, will be happy for the respite after dragging his master halfway across France.

Although from North Africa, Francois Pierre, like his almost namesake, Jean Pierre, had also once been a pirate. But that was many years ago, in a different world, before naval treaties and the rise of the privateering forces made life before the mast too dangerous. If you asked either man now, they'd both tell you it was a fool-hardy endeavour, best left to younger men, if at all.

Jean Pierre is struck by how old his old comrade-in-arms looks. Perhaps he'd see the same thing in himself if he bothered to go near a mirror. The old Barbary Pirate walks with a pronounced limp that was not there before. Despite his clear ill-health, he smiles a half-toothed smile at Jean Pierre and calls out, "Jean Pierre, you old sea-snake, are you still alive? You won't believe it, but I was just thinking about our adventures in Nassau. Good times indeed. You still living in that den of thieves they call Paris?"

"Francois, you salty sea dog, I am indeed. Thankfully I'm far enough away from its centre to avoid the stench, but close enough that I may still take advantage of her infinite charms. Despite life's constant challenges I confess I thought I had found peace of a sort. It really is good to see you, old friend."

"Peace, eh? Ah yes, my good friend Jean. I can tell you a story or two about this thing you call peace." He spits the word as though it were a bug that has foolishly flown into his mouth. "I like not this hellish state of immobility and decay that I have descended into. I am dying slowly. The cancer is in my bones you see, and the state I find myself in is not worthy of the man I once was. Peace? No! I would not even wish it on those tax-collecting pigs who try to extort me. I gave them peace for their troubles. They now rest in peace under that pine tree over there." He gestures with a crooked, hairy finger in some direction.

"No, I think a fierce and proper death at the end of a cutlass might be a truer end for men like us. I long for the sport of it. Let us go inside and reminisce about how we survived a fiendish past, and risk giving away our age.

"Now, to what do I owe the honour of this visit? I think I have some of that good rum from Saint-Domingue hidden away for special occasions. We'll warm our old bones by the fire and talk about old times."

They sit together in a small front room at a rickety little table in front of a small fireplace and toast to seeing each other after all these years. The walls are adorned with the hunting paraphernalia from a thousand hunts, as well as the heads of several deer and, oddly, a huge catfish.

"Ah, that," says Francois, seemingly pleased that the grotesque thing has caught the attention of his friend.

Perhaps you do you not remember old friend. It's a souvenir from our expedition to the São Francisco river in Brazil. I think you were wounded at the time and perhaps remained aboard the ship. Anyway, that monster fed us all while we hid from the British in the jungle. Three-hundred pounds it must have weighed. The Indians called it *Jaú*, although I'm not sure that that means.

"But enough about fish. What about you? You're a long way from home old friend."

"Alas, my errand is an unhappy one. A letter… I mean, I received a letter from my beloved Anna … there's a child, a boy… a son. I never suspected and she never said a word. Until now. After her parents drove me away, I feared I would never see her again. Even though I knew in my heart that I'd never forget her as long as I lived. And now she's dying. That's what the letter was about. She asked me to come. That's where I'm going."

From the way the words tumble out it's clear that Jean Pierre has still not yet fully processed the news.

"You and I, Francois, we don't deserve love unless bought from ladies of ill repute. Perhaps you were luckier — you had a mother and a father. But I never knew such love. I never did understand why you felt the call of the sea. You had your own reasons no doubt, and a man's secret must remain his own until he wishes to share his burden with a friend. I have never trusted my secrets to anyone, not even a man in a cassock. And now I find I have a secret that is so secret not even I knew of it. Forgive the rambling old friend, it feels good to unburden myself to a trusted ally for once.

"I had a choice once long ago. Kill her family and hope she would forgive me. Or leave and hope she would remember me. I made my choice and I don't regret it. But a son…," his voice trails off, and they sit for a moment in awkward silence.

It's Francois who breaks the spell. "You were a different man. We both were. You must forgive yourself. Now drink, I think you'll find the rum quite forgiving too."

At this they laugh.

And then Jean Pierre says, "I certainly hope so. For I fear my troubles may only just be beginning. I had to kill a man on the road, and now I dread that further misfortune cannot be far behind."

Ambush! Jean Pierre faces off with the DuClerc clan.

CHAPTER 4

Rum

"Yo-ho-ho, and a bottle of rum."
Robert Louis Stevenson

At the Congress of Cracow in 1364, King Peter I of Cyprus brought with him a special new alcoholic spirit to impress the assembled kings, monarchs, and nobles of Europe. The drink was a powerful elixir produced from fermented and distilled molasses of sugarcane, which was plentiful in Cyprus during that time. This rum, as it became known, proved to be a big hit, even standing out amidst the lavish setting of the Congress, with some going as far as to describe it as being such a splendid drink as to be capable of exorcising the demons from whomever partook of it.

Such was its popularity in Cracow that it didn't take long before the legendary drink, ironically made from the simplest of plants, was on the lips and palates of the rest of Europe's high society.

Almost a hundred years later, Prince Henry of Portugal would introduce that same simple plant to the island of Madeira. There it would become the liquid that fuelled not only the Portuguese economy, but that of much of Europe. Moreover, the island's location proved to be a strategically significant stop for many of Europe's trade routes, and it wasn't long before sugarcane found its way west across the Atlantic Ocean. By the 1700s the French had expanded the sugar trade to the French Caribbean Islands. The island of Saint-Domingue, known today as Haiti, became the centre of the sugar universe.

From there it's not hard to make the leap to rum production. And despite a prohibition against its production and trade in continental France, rum became a highly sought-after commodity and spawned a smuggling industry among the many merchants and pirates who plied their trade in the warm, thirsty waters of the Caribbean.

Thanks to a favourable location, rich climate and yellow, fertile soil, Saint-Domingue was home to some of the finest plantations and distilleries in all of the Antilles. The island was the perfect ecosystem for rum, which would begin its delicious journey as delicate little green sugarcane shoots to be nurtured with dung and natural mulch and left to grow for up to eighteen months. Once they had reached a height of around eight feet, the mature canes were carefully trimmed of all their leaves and taken to the mill. There they were then crushed, and the precious juices extracted.

The juice was boiled in giant cast-iron boilers, where it seethed and bubbled and evaporated, until only a thick syrup remained. This was poured into a cooling tank where it cooled to form a shiny, protective crystalline crust, which, once removed, revealed the precious molasses underneath, ready to be boiled again before being allowed to ferment.

What was left was the poetic heart of distillation process, the *coeur de chauffe*. This was heated again and the alcoholic vapour condensed and collected. Only then was the final product transferred to wooden barrels and aged to give it colour and additional flavour.

*

* *

The two Pierres sit together warming their outsides by the little fire and their insides with Saint-Domingue rum. The approaching cold of night brings with it old tales and resurrects forgotten names. It also brings two hearty appetites.

The master of the house presents a stew to match; rabbit, hung for five days precisely to coax out the subtle flavour, along with potatoes, carrots and wild herbs, all languishing in a gravy made from the animal's own blood and seasoned liberally with black peppercorns.

Jean Pierre had forgotten about the hidden culinary talents of his friend but is now inclined to think that his old comrade had perhaps acquired a bit too strong a liking for the spiciness of the latter ingredient in his adventures in the Americas. The fiery pepper makes him sweat, despite the cold. Even with his mouth on fire, though, there's no disputing the deliciousness of the food.

They eat in silence until Francois notices that Pierre's rum is finished. He gets up to refill both glasses and enquires in an offhand way about the trip – the road, old Luc, the number of travellers – in his own diplomatic way, he's trying to get to the subject Pierre had broached briefly previously – the unfortunate meeting with the bandits.

"Mm hmm," replies the other with a mouthful of rabbit and potato, "Luc? Oh, still strong as an ox. Perhaps there is some gypsy magic at work with old beast."

"And on the other matter?"

Jean Pierre recounts the action in some detail, giving as close a description as he can of the men involved in the attack.

Francois eyes him across the little table for a moment. Swills his rum. Takes a sip and then speaks.

"Jean, my old and great friend, I fear that you have killed one of the sons of the notorious Swiss fugitive, DuClerc. He and his family of scurvy dogs have been a pox on these parts for no small time now, terrorising the village people and waylaying travellers on the roads and very often killing them. They know better than to mess with on old wolf like me – the sons are nothing more than dim-witted villains with only half a brain between them. But their father is a different animal. He'll want revenge. If he's followed you or learned of your whereabouts, your trip may end sooner than you had planned."

A look of defiance flickers across Jean's face. But it's to no avail. Francois is adamant. Any further discussion on the matter is closed. "No, you will leave here before dawn, and I shall make sure that you are not followed."

"My dear Francois, I do not wish you to go to war with your neighbours on my behalf. Either I leave now, our we face them together."

Here a smile creeps across Francois' lips. "No, my dear friend. Perhaps you have brought not trouble, but rather, a gift. I would like nothing better to fight alongside you again, but perhaps this is not the way today. Now, let us hide your wagon so that we may get a good night's rest. Tomorrow we shall follow my plan. You will continue on your important errand, and I shall take care of the rest. It will be my pleasure. Perhaps I shall not die in my bed after all."

*

* *

They're up at four the next morning, Francois with a glint in his eye and Jean Pierre with the look of a man who has resolved to finish what he has started. As the sound of Luc's hooves recede into the distance, Francois readies himself to enact his part of the plan.

Perhaps he has been anticipating this moment, for on a nearby fig tree, someone has nailed planks to form a makeshift series of steps reaching up into the leafy canopy. The fig leaves are broad and dense enough to hide a man if he remains still enough.

As the sun begins to rise Francois climbs the trunk and curses his knees, imagining a time when he could fly up the main mast of schooner faster than the rats who were their constant companions on the vessels.

Nevertheless, he lodges himself in a crook between two large branches and checks his weaponry. Aside from the two machetes that he has strategically placed a short distance from the base of the tree, he has two long muskets, loaded and locked, and a pair of French duelling pistols tucked into the old belt he wears about his waist.

We don't know how far Jean Pierre manages to travel before he hears the unmistakable bark of the flintlocks behind him.

Gunfire gives way to the cadent clip-clop of Luc's hooves on the dusty path. The Kingdoms of Italy lie ahead.

Jean Pierre with weapons at the ready.

CHAPTER 5

In the footsteps of Hannibal

"Piano piano si va lontano."
Ancient axiom.

Dark thunderclouds of discontent gather on Europe's political horizon. Relationships between the kingdoms of Austria, Prussia, France and the various Italian dominions are constantly in flux, with feuds and alliances changing with the wind. There is also the great sleeping Bear of Russia to consider, whose unnecessary awakening could add further seasoning to this already dangerous stew of uncertainty. Something unspoken simmers beneath the surface.

It's a most dangerous time for travellers who dare to venture beyond the reaches and protection of the castles, towns and villages. Crossing paths with unknown groups on the road can mean death for one side or the other, or both, in a spasm of mutual destruction. It's best to avoid such encounters if possible. But sometimes there's no alternative, and in such cases, it's best to hope that lady luck is on your side.

The danger is especially acute in the border regions, where nationalists of all persuasions exist in a posture of default hostility towards each other and anybody else who wanders into their territory.

This is what's going through Jean Pierre's mind as he looks at the snow-covered Alps rising majestically into the sky in the distance. Beautiful and dangerous. Along with the early warning system that is old Luc's neighing, he has a small marine telescope, which he now deploys in service of surveying the way ahead. He'd rather not kill anyone else before he reaches his destination, if he can avoid it. But as we have already seen, he will if he must.

Despite being armed to the teeth, with weapons at the ready, the surprise encounter with DuClerc is more than enough for one journey. Luckily, so far, the only other souls he'd come across were an abbot and his two security guards on horseback, as well as two pages who followed along on foot.

For reasons of discretion, Jean Pierre sticks to the less well-trodden routes, making good time. But now, as the path gets steeper and winds higher, and as the air gets icier, there is another consideration. A wheel might break, or worse, Old Luc could slip and break a leg. He has no choice but to slow down.

He's covered Luc's limbs with cloth and leather windings to protect the animal's legs and hooves from the sharp rocks. This has the added benefit of muffling their sound somewhat. But the going is hard.

Below the snow line, great forests close them in and Jean Pierre has to cut through fallen branches with his heavy

German machete. Above the snow line they struggle through icy fields deep enough to scrape the underside of the wagon.

The mountain is a giant dragon's back that forced itself out of the bowels of the earth more than sixty-five million years ago. An icy fortification where winds swirl in all directions at once, and where careless travellers are in constant danger of losing their way, or worse, their lives. But across and over this mountain he must go. So, he drives himself forward carefully, and with a due sense of his mission.

Dawn breaks on the eastern side of this prehistoric formation, blessing Jean Pierre's face with welcome sunshine. The ice is smoother here, and within a few hours it gives way to firmer, stonier ground. The bindings about Luc's hooves have all but disintegrated and Jean Pierre can hear the distinctive clink of horseshoes on rock. But the tireless quadruped pushes on, pulling behind it the creaking cart that, despite the punishment it has endured as it bounced and jolted across the unforgiving terrain, along with its bearings, is miraculously still in one piece.

Passing into lower altitudes where the topography mellows into undulating hills, he recognises that he is finally in Italy.

You, me, and Hannibal, eh? he half thinks, half says to Luc, imagining another crossing, almost two-thousand years previous, when a famous Carthaginian general led his army of thousands of infantry and cavalry, and a troop of elephants, across the Alps, in order to strike at the very heart of a hegemonic Roman Republic.

If you went any slower, Luc, we'd freeze to death. The animal snorts and paws the ground, perhaps in acknowledgement, perhaps just to expose a tuft of grass to eat.

Jean Pierre gives silent thanks to an ancient guardian angel who has long protected this duo of man and horse on their many adventures together, both dangerous and unwise. Hannibal's reason for the crossing was war. Jean Pierre's is a missive from the past; a great love that should never have been forgotten.

His thoughts turn now to the contents of the letter, and a time long ago. A wry smile tugs at the corner of his lips. Would this simple piece of paper be enough to grant him access where all those years ago he would have been met with hot lead from a musket? How ironic. Laetitia's father had made it quite clear at the time that Jean Pierre was not welcome. The old man made a great song and dance about being a distinguished gent, with a certain rank in society. But he was also a stubborn and vain man, who would not countenance his daughter consorting with a pirate. In retrospect, perhaps it was only right and proper that the father had wanted to protect his daughter.

On a particular day at a time in the distant past, the old man had confronted Jean Pierre, politely, but with loaded pistol in hand, and had informed him in no uncertain terms that his daughter would leave the protection of his hearth and home only with a suitor worthy of her station in life. Jean Pierre's past made him a man singularly unfit to meet those conditions. He was to leave and never come back.

Jean Pierre for his part had been confused and heartbroken. Perhaps it was true – that a man with as rotten a history as his was indeed unworthy of such an honourable family. His own family had disintegrated even longer ago than he could remember. It is but a vague and terrible memory, best suppressed, as it had been for many moons.

He cannot recall much about his father, other than that he had been a nasty drunk who beat and tormented both mother and son.

In this dark and stormy former time, on an equally dark and stormy night, the demon alcohol had overtaken his father, who had prowled the house lashing out at everybody and everything in his path. The mother had naturally borne the brunt of this cantankerousness.

Anger had swallowed Pierre's being as though drowning him. In the madness of the moment, he had leapt upon his father and strangled the life out of him. Not content with the limp body in his hands he had smashed the man's head against the cobbled floor, again and again and again, until the blood had run freely into the cracks between the stones. In the aftermath of this violence, Jean Pierre had had a vision of a hundred versions of his immediate future, none of them good.

His biggest worry directly following the incident had been the local militia, a force corrupted to very core, and one that was allied to the now dead man. No, his only plausible escape had been just that; to run, to flee, to hide.

He had donned the clothes of a servant and made his way to the port of Paris, where he had hoped to find safe passage to anyplace where he was not known. There he had hidden behind a tavern, waiting for his opportunity. But word of his crime was already in the air, and rather than risk being discovered, he had stolen onto the nearest vessel and stowed away.

His plan had seemed perfectly sound until that point. It had been his choice of ship that set his course upon the tides of fate. It was a pirate vessel bound for Nassau. When the crew found him, they had given him a choice; prove his worth by steel or learn to float. He had chosen the former, and although not an accomplished swordsman, had managed to best his opponent in a fair fight. The dead man was thrown overboard, and Jean Pierre was welcomed into his new family. The captain of the ship also found in him other useful skills – the ability to interpret and calculate numbers, as well as to read and write.

Jean Pierre had spent five years before the mast, looting, plundering, and learning the wild ways of a pirate. Until returning to Paris, where he had vowed to change his destiny and forsake the life of piracy forever.

Back in France, he had enlisted in the French army and soon found himself in a regiment tasked with quelling popular uprisings at the vanguard of France's territorial ambitions. It was while escorting one of the many generals on a visit to Northern Piedmont that he had met Laetitia. Being still relatively young, and love being what it is, he had requested a discharge from the army to make a life with the new love of his life. Alas, it was not to be. He soon found that he could not outrun his past. Memories and tongues can be cruel to a man trying to erase a chequered past. A villager had recognised Jean Pierre in a market and told his story to the girl's father.

Despite the ex-pirate's remonstrations and promises that that life was behind him, no amount of explanation or goodwill could change the old man's disposition on the matter, and he never could bring himself to see both sides of the story.

Jean Pierre had made the hardest decision he had ever had to make on that rainy day. He accepted the father's demand to leave, not out of respect to the man, but for the love of Laetitia. He could have cut the man down like so much sugarcane. But he had chosen a peaceful course on that day in which even God showed her disapproval by pelting the earth with a hailstorm of almost biblical proportions.

As he left the woman he loved and made his way back to France, Filipe's father never dreamed that Laetitia carried his son in her womb.

And now the man who had forsaken his love to become a potato farmer, had left his potato farm to once again seek out the woman he had loved so much.

Filipe, aged approximately seven.

CHAPTER 6

A grandfather's influence

"It might take a year, it might take a day, but
what's meant to be will always find a way."
Unknown

Filipe Borriana Francisconi was not unlike other boys of his age and socio-economic environment. Tough circumstances had made him independent and self-sufficient. Ever since he could remember, he had been responsible for working the small farm near the village of San Giuseppe, where he lived with his mother and grandfather – the only father figure he'd ever known – minding the pigs, milking the three dairy cows, feeding the chickens and tending to the vegetable garden that formed the basis of their communal subsistence. He was also an adept fisherman and a fair hunter of small game for the family table.

Filipe's mother was an undeniable source of his happiness, the reverse also being true, since the two of them were blessed with a relationship in which they were not only mother and son, but also great friends. He loved nothing more than to see her smile after a hard day's toil and know that it was the fruit of a genuine and deep connection that perhaps only mothers who love their sons will ever really know.

On those days spent hunting wild pigs or hares, Filipe would be sure to wash himself and his prey in the icy waters of the nearby stream so as not to drag mud into the house out of respect for both mother and grandfather.

The grandfather for his part was a stern man, but he was also a great mentor and role model for the boy who must later become a man of good character, even though his own father had been torn from their lives by a pernicious world.

Together the three of them made the best of the situation, living in relative harmony with each other and their surroundings.

When the boy was around seven years old, he was summoned to his grandfather's bedside, where the old man lay dying of an ancient and cruel disease that was not widely understood in those days, which we today know as cancer. Through fits and coughs the old man was able to communicate one last time with the boy. He spoke some words that were too soft for anyone else to hear and bestowed upon Filipe his prized prototype Crespi breech-loader. The gift was an apt analogy to the relationship that had developed between the man and the boy in the latter's short years, being simultaneously dangerous and affectionate beyond measure. The boy was now truly the man of the house. Provider and protector.

Filipe learnt another lesson that day. The priest who attended the final passing of grandfather Francisconi, perhaps seeing an opportunity to proselytise to a young and impressionable soul, underestimated the young man and came on too strong. In the face of death, Filipe came to understand that there was a difference between Christian behaviour and living in perpetual fear of a capricious, gloating being in Heaven, who somehow adjudicated all matters, and could simply snuff out a life without any kind of satisfactory explanation.

Afterward his mother had tried to console the boy, saying that sometimes even good people were taken by the Hand of the Divine before their time. Did he not notice that as the grandfather closed his eyes for a final time, a wind started to blow? "The wind carries the souls of the good to a better place. When the sun rises tomorrow, your grandfather will have joined your grandmother in Heaven."

Filipe cried, realising that he would never see his grandfather again. Never see the man, who despite his gruffness, was the boy's hero. Never hear the eloquent stories of his military days in Biella. Never receive any more of the advice and life-lessons that were the greatest gift the old man had given the boy.

No. His grandfather was dead. And if God had anything to do with it, then he was angry at God.

At least he still had his mother.

*

* *

But disease it seems, is never content. There came a Sunday following the death of the grandfather, at an indeterminate time in the mind of the young Filipe, who was still at an age when time didn't follow the same path that it did with adults, when there was no sermon for the villagers to hear at the local church. The priest instead appeared at the Francisconi home to minister to the dying mother. Alas, the woman was labouring under the same illness that had taken the grandfather.

The sensation was almost too much to bear for a boy who had yet to reach puberty. He asked the priest if God would not instead take him and spare his mother. The priest was about to respond, but the mother managed to interject, "Filipe, dear son of mine. You are but a boy, with a great future ahead of you. I am not dead yet, but I will go to my maker happy in the knowledge that you will be happy one day, with children of your own, and perhaps even grandchildren. Now, hush with such nonsense. When the time comes, honour my memory by being strong."

In his bewilderment, he thought he saw his mother press a small envelope into priest's hand. Why would his mother be sending a letter now? And to whom?

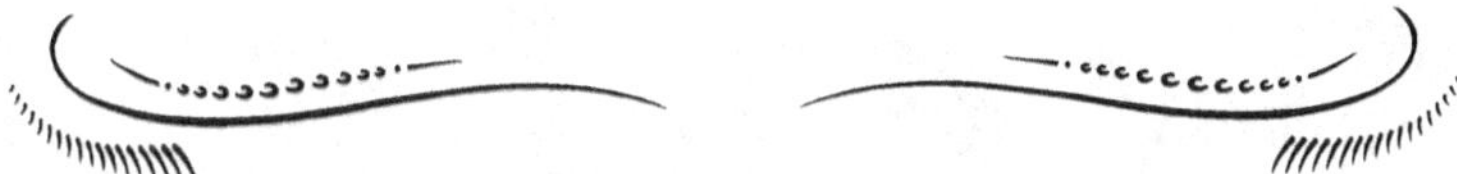

Filipe sights down the barrel.

CHAPTER 7

A mother's death

"There is something about losing a mother that is permanent
and inexpressible—a wound that will never quite heal."
Susan Wiggs

While diplomatic relations between France and Italy
remained nominal, on the ground things were a lot different.
A murmur carried on the wind, whispered softly into ears on
both sides of the border. The word it spoke was War!

In the border regions, where communities rubbed up
against each other, interdependent, yet in competition for the
same resources, a certain realpolitik played out. Residents of
both sides were weary of confronting each other across the
fields and rivers that separated them. Staying hidden is often
the best way to avoid trouble, and this comes naturally to a
young hunter.

*

**

Against this backdrop we find Filipe moving quietly
through the undergrowth along the banks of the Torrente

Cenischia. What noise he does make, is easily covered by the rushing of the stream, which at this time of year is experiencing its normal autumn discharge. He's carrying a small deer that he killed earlier, and gutted, using an armadillo-tail-handled knife that was among his grandfather's belongings, along with the Crespi breech-loader and an ammunition pouch.

He's about to turn southwards and head for home when he spots two soldiers on the far side of the river, fresh from a looting spree, so far as he can tell. It's not uncommon to see militia of both sides taking liberties with the local population, so Filipe isn't overly concerned. It's better, he decides, to leave them to their own devices.

Until he hears the scream.

He freezes and crouches lower. Squinting through the leaves to get a better look, he sees that there's a woman lying on the ground alongside the men. Her clothes are torn and there she appears to have blood running from her nose. She's begging the two men to let her go.

At this juncture Filipe decides to act. He knows it would be best to retreat quietly, but he cannot countenance this atrocity. What he is about to do goes against all the teachings he knows, but the woman's life is in danger. All he can think is that the woman might well have been his mother.

Filipe takes the Crespi from his shoulder and quietly loads it, all the while keeping an eye on the scene that's unfolding across the way. As he closes the breechblock, he touches a finger to his tongue and passes it across the sight, a habit he inherited from his grandfather, who taught him how to hunt. The routine is almost subconscious now; perhaps it focusses his mind and improves his aim.

Finding a spot to shoot from, he lies down and places a cloth on a rock to support the barrel and stop it getting scratched when the recoil pushes it back. Tucking the butt into his shoulder, he sights down the barrel and breathes in a long, slow breath.

He aims between the eyes of the soldier closest to him - a ruddy, red-haired brute - and thinks to himself, aim true, so that the game does not suffer, as his grandfather always used to instruct him. This dictum has served him well, and now he feels himself applying the same cold principles to the terrible task in front of him. The choice to kill had come surprisingly easy, perhaps a trait inherited from a father whom he never knew.

And then he breathes out in a long, smooth, steady, gentle exhale, feeling his heartbeat slow, just as his grandfather had taught him. His index finger begins to squeeze…

A hand taps him lightly on the shoulder.

He tenses and swears under his breath whatever swear-words a young man knows how to swear. Foolish, he could have been killed.

"Shhh," comes a voice.

Filipe smiles. There's only one other creature of the woods who could be as silent as he could be. Rubens, his friend from countless hunts and adventures in the hills.

Without taking his eye off the prey he whispers, "Rubens, you are in the way, There's a woman in danger. I need to save her from those filthy French bastards. They will taste the lead from my gun."

"Yes, my friend, I see that, but perhaps it's best that you are not the trigger for war against France. We don't know who that woman is; it could be a trap. And besides, you have only one ball, and there are two of them. keep your wits about you and you will keep your head."

Rubens lowers himself to the ground, shoulder to shoulder with his friend, and speaks in a sombre tone, "Leave the soldiers for another day. I have some delicate news to tell you, your mother fears her end is very near, and has called for you to be at her side. We must get home…" And with that he wiggles backwards like a weasel, away from their vantage point looking across the river, and disappears behind a thicket.

Without saying a word, Filipe does the same, and they begin the heavy-hearted march home. The wind that had accompanied him when he set off that morning now swirls around them like a harbinger of bad news. It had been no secret that Filipe's mother was in poor health, but it was never easy when the time came.

Rubens accompanies him in silence, as friends do at such times. He thinks that if, perhaps, he had been from southern Italy, he would have known what to say. Southerners always had such an easy way with words, being simply more outgoing than their northern cousins. Or if he had been a politician. Politicians also always had a lot to say.

On the other hand, being quiet has its merits, too.

They descend a rocky promontory and follow the stream as it cascades into the valley, where they soon find themselves on a wide plain surrounded by coniferous trees that stretch their limbs above the bracken and ferns that are so typical of the area. After a while they turn away from the river and make their way through the now browning grasslands until they emerge some three-hundred meters from Filipe's home.

To his surprise, Filipe sees that a strange cart in the robust French style circa 17th century has taken up residence on the small track leading to the farmhouse. As out of place as the cart might be, it's no less unusual than the strange horse that stands nearby, and which is undoubtedly the business-end of the conveyance. Although clearly old, the horse has the strong, sturdy legs characteristic of a French Breton draught horse.

The final resting place of Filipe's mother.

CHAPTER 8

A funeral

"There are no goodbyes for us.
Wherever you are, you will always be in my heart."
Mahatma Gandhi

The uneducated beast has been blithely munching away at the flowerbeds that his mother had so lovingly tended over the summer. The animal is no doubt hungry after whatever journey has brought him here, because the roses, dandelions and pumpkin flowers have all been decapitated. Now the horse appears to be working his way through the rest of anything that looks even vaguely green or juicy. The quadruped is no fool, though, since it has avoided the poisonous horsetails. Just as well that the buttercups and other toxic plants are out of reach behind the small fence in the back pasture.

Filipe has the urge to give the horse a swift slap on the flanks for its trouble, but decides that he has more pressing priorities, such as going to his mother. And speaking of slaps, whoever left the horse untethered certainly also deserves a slap to their flanks for being so disrespectful of his mother's garden.

He enters the house and hastily leaves his rifle and other paraphernalia on the rustic kitchen table, where someone has left a wild hare and a brace of quails, along with a veritable thicket of chanterelle mushrooms. The kitchen represents a happy memory for Filipe, having spent many hours here with his mother, baking garlic bread and concocting great pots of chicken cacciatore, the recipe for which, legend has it, was perfected by his grandmother. Boy and mother were great habitués of the kitchen, where they cooked up simple, honest cuisine using whatever grew in their garden, as well as that most important of ingredients, love.

Rubens shouts a cursory goodbye, but knowing that Filipe is beyond hearing him, simply turns to retrieve the deer from the front of the house where they had dumped it upon their arrival. Best to give Filipe his space at this moment. Filipe for his part feels an almost psychic pull that draws his legs towards his mother's bedroom.

Aside from the familiar personage of Father Pinarello, there is another, unknown man in the room, leaning over his mother who is lying in the bed. The man gives off an air of quiet strength, his strong features almost noble but for the many scars that line his face and hands. Curiously the strange man holds his mother's hands tenderly in his, and she, in return reaches up to push the man's hair away from his cheek, where her hand rests in a gesture of affection that leaves Filipe at once bewildered and angry.

An icy pang of jealousy grips the boy's heart. Who is this interloper that he holds such sway over his mother? He sits down next to the priest, who prays quietly while telling the beads on a well-worn rosary.

The stranger seems to notice the boy's presence, for he kisses the mother lightly on the forehead and turns to face Filipe.

His mother calls him to her side, saying, "Filipe, this is your father." Filipe the boy wants to scream in anger. Filipe the hunter remains poised like a coiled spring.

"I can only imagine how much of a shock this must be for you. His name is Jean Pierre. Would that you might have met him before, but there were forces that worked strongly against this outcome. Mistakes and sorrows of the past must be forgotten. The future may belong to God, but it is up to men to walk the path.

"I am leaving this earth, no doubt. I pray you will become good friends. You are my fruit. It was with great love that you came into the world. I daresay we had a good and happy life together, but just as the fruit separates from the tree, so, too, must you separate from me. Your father…" Here she hesitates for a moment and coughs a raspy cough, wiping her mouth quickly with a handkerchief in the hopes that no-one will see the small flecks of blood. But Filipe's watchful eyes miss nothing, and he is scared and confused.

The strange man's hard features soften as he looks at his newly acquainted son with a look of great tenderness. The scars that once spoke of a life in the shadows, now emanate the kind pain that is most closely associated with deep love.

The mother continues, "you will not stay here on this land after today, my son. The farm has been sold; the money is in that leather bag. It is yours, but I have given it to your father for safekeeping. You will live with your father in France, or wherever the two of you decide to go. You will become a man, take a wife and have children of your own. You will make a life worthy of that which your grandfather and I imagined for you. I have prayed every day since you were born that your life would be blessed, and I have no doubt it will be so."

Tears flow from all eyes present. Even the stoic priest, who is used to dealing with loss and death allows a tear to run down his cheek before quickly wiping it away with the sleeve of his cassock. He had become a friend to the woman over many years through his interactions with her in the village, and knew her to be a generous and good-hearted soul.

Amongst the hot tears that punctuate the anguish-filled air of the little room, Filipe finds his voice, "Mother! It's not possible. God is playing tricks on us. You can't leave me. You can't. We will go to the capital to find a cure."

"My son, the physicians would only bleed me and take away what little money we have. Besides, God does not play tricks, that is blasphemy, my time has simply come. No more, no less," her voice is getting weaker, and now she beckons to Jean Pierre to bring his ear closer to her mouth. Jean Pierre takes her left hand in his two hands and the boy does the same on other side of the bed. "Jean Pierre, this is Filipe, the son you never knew. Our beautiful son. Promise me that you will take care of each other."

Jean Pierre can only nod silently. The guilt of having forsaken mother and child still consumes him.

"Filipe, your father will love and respect you, just as you must love and respect him. When I pass, as I soon must, promise me that you will be more than just father and son." She asks for a clean handkerchief and coughs up obvious puffs of blood. "Dear ones, now leave me to rest. Please open the window so that my soul may have unhindered passage from this place."

With that she closes her eyes, and her breathing slows and gets shallower and shallower until she exhibits no movement. She crosses quietly onto the other side, like an angel finally resting after a grand battle, with an enigmatic yet peaceful smile upon her face. Neither pirate nor hunter can hide their sorrow, and both weep silently without looking at each other.

*
* *

No one can sleep that night, save for short periods when fatigue draws its cloudy curtain behind eyelids that are being held tightly closed. Filipe sees the stranger, his father, get up several time and pray by the side of his now departed mother. But he remains silent and still until he hears the unmistakable chorus of the birds announcing the dawn, and the sun casting yellow beams through the uneven rectangles of the small windows.

The priest, who had kept his own vigil during the night, now greets a group of black-clad figures who have mysteriously arrived from places unknown. Presumably, an unction of undertakers from one of the bigger nearby towns.

They begin their preparations as quietly and swiftly as they arrived. First clearing the small room where the body lies, so that they can undress and wash the corpse, all the while chanting good things about the life of the woman, to advocate for her safe passage to heaven among the angels who are certain to be in attendance. A coffin has not been prepared, so a shroud will have to do, but this is not uncommon during these times.

All protocol observed, the body is brought to the small graveyard on the hill behind the homestead, where someone has dug a reasonable grave beside the two other headstones belonging to Filipe's grandfather and grandmother.

The enclosed plot itself had been constructed by the grandfather many years ago upon the death of his wife, and now stands under a large oak. The magnificent tree will provide shade and protection for Filipe's mother who had loved to sit under its twisted branches, just as it had for his grandparents in days gone by. It's a fitting final resting place.

The formalities of the burial over, the small gathering disperses, leaving father and son alone at the graveside. The two embrace as though they have known each other all their lives. The loss of a loved one has created a communion between them that has grown strong, even though it's barely a matter of days since they were first made aware of each other's existence.

Jean Pierre begins to shovel dirt into the hole, on top of the tightly shrouded body. Filipe, on the other side of the grave, begins to secure the headstone using splinters of rock to wedge the granite upright and prevent it from toppling over.

Finally, they both place heavy flagstones on top of the newly filled in grave, creating a secure tomb that cannot be easily disturbed by the many hungry animals that roam wild in this bucolic setting. Despite the sadness of the occasion, man and boy are pleased with their work, having fulfilled their role in bringing a little peace and relief to the aching hearts that lingered there.

Standing side by side, they say a quiet prayer, and then turn towards the homestead. Filipe gazes down upon the little house, knowing that this is probably the last time he will do so.

And then they set about making their own preparations to leave. Jean Pierre hitches old Luc to the wagon, just as he had done weeks prior. Luc whinnies and scrapes his front foot, knowing that this will elicit the usual carrot or other treat from his master. The old beast stands happily masticating and whipping its tail absent-mindedly, thinking only horsey thoughts, unaware of the human drama that has been playing out around him.

Filipe for his part finds an old trunk and gathers the things that are important to him. The money from the sale of his mother's lands, clothes, his trusty machete, the armadillo-tail-handled skinning knife, his grandfather's rifles, and of course, the Crespi. In the kitchen he fills his leather satchel with his favourite cooking knives, a sharpening steel and two small copper pots.

Two neighbours have gathered up what remained of the mother's clothes to be donated to the church, while the priest seems to be in charge of preparing the farmhouse for its new inhabitants.

Rubens appears, bringing pieces of smoked venison, dried sausages and cured cheeses for the journey. The two speak briefly, with Rubens assuring his friend that if he ever decides to come back, he has a friend and a welcome hearth. "You know where my home is," he declares.

Filipe answers in a brave voice, "Yes, Rubens, I will never forget you or this place."

And with that, the party of two men and one horse sets off on the return journey to France, and the beginning of new adventure. Sometime later, Filipe twists his small body and looks back, exhaling a deep sigh, almost as though he hasn't breathed for a while. One day I will be back to reclaim what is mine and restore the memory of my mother and grandfather, he thinks to himself.

Jean Pierre, intuiting his young travelling companion's mind, speaks now for the first time since they left the little farmhouse behind. "Son my land is already yours. You will become a man fast, and you will know what your wishes really are, and these will lead you to your next steps. If you want to you can come back here. Or if you like you can stay in France. Let time tell you what to do."

They continue their long journey in silence, listening only to the trot and happy snorting of the old equine, a new friend for Felipe, who has forgiven the horse for eating the flowers that now seem so insignificant in the grand scheme of things.

Father and son wait in absolute stillness.

CHAPTER 9

Ambush

The weeks-long trip is ample time for the father and son to get acquainted. As Luc picks his way through the landscape with an uncanny sense of direction, both man and boy begin to feel more comfortable breaking the silences that are inevitably becoming shorter between them with each passing mile.

Filipe asks where they are going, and what their future will be like. After all, until recently he had no idea that a father even existed.

Jean Pierre feels pride at how his son seems to be opening up; his posture, speech and attitude are those of a young man on his way to adulthood. "You know, my son...well...first, it is important for you to know that I have always dreamed of having a son. I am truly sorry that we have only come together under sad circumstances. But now we shall make the best of it.

"Perhaps it was for the best that your mother and your grandfather kept you in the dark about your father. They had their reasons. It is true that I led an undignified life for many years before I met your mother. Your grandfather once said that I had the blood of Cain. I only understood his meaning with the Christian influence of you mother.

"Indeed, you mother delivered me from Hell, Dante's land of limbo and lost souls. She gave my life newfound meaning. She was truly the great love of my life before I was cruelly driven away.

"But that is of course not the whole story." Here he pauses, perhaps considering whether he should go on.

"You see, Filipe, long before I met your mother, I was the son of a respectable man; a man of status and ownership; accountant to nobles; but he was also a man of countless evils and cruelty towards my mother and me. I killed him for it. It was not premeditated, but it would have been impossible to for me to account for my actions under the circumstances in which it happened. My father's associates would never have forgiven me, and even my own brother would have been glad of one less man with whom to share my father's possessions, were I to have been arrested. It was an event that set the world against me. I had to flee.

"By chance I found myself on a pirate-ship headed for the Americas. I became one of them and spent years repeating the same horrible crimes that had set me against the world in the first instance. I rose to become second in command of the ship, to a man by the name Captain Edward Thatch, a depraved Englishman who claimed to have been born in a dark corner of London that even the devil was afraid to visit.

"Alcohol and the devil joined forces, taking me on a dark adventure that consumed my soul and concealed the light from me.

"One day, while attacking a Portuguese ship off the coast of Brazil I became aware that our adversaries were not the fighters or navy cutthroats I believed them to be. Instead, they were women and children and a crew of freed black slaves. We were the rum-fuelled aggressors, and they were merely defending their lives against us. The sight of all those corpses littering the deck was enough to awaken me from my long and violent nightmare.

"Captain Thatch was still smiling and boasting among the bodies, mightily pleased with his latest conquest, when I stabbed him through the heart with my cutlass. He retched blood and died on the deck like a stuck pig. At that precise moment the dark clouds parted, and a beam of light illuminated my features.

"My compatriots rounded on me, no doubt to avenge their captain, but the third mate, a Berber who had taken the name Francois Pierre, intervened. Raising his arms, he shouted, 'Hail the new captain,' and a cheer went up. Before anyone could change their minds, I broached the ship's rum supplies and gave the men their fill. The very next day, I commanded our return to France.

"We arrived without incident in the Port of La Rochelle, where I attempted to hand control of the vessel to my only friend on board, Francois Pierre, but he had made up his mind to forsake piracy along with me. We both knew that we were breaking the code of brotherhood by abandoning our comrades, but our course was set.

"That night, we made off with a goodly amount of treasure and gold coin and disappeared without alerting the crew.

"We had hoped that that would be the end of it, after all there was still a significant stash of booty aboard the ship; more than enough that no one would notice what we had taken with us.

"It was not to be. Nigh half a year later, a faction from the original crew tracked me down to the very land that I had bought for myself with my ill-gotten gains. How they found me is a mystery

"There were five of them. They must have waited in the fields until dark, for it was late when I heard them surrounding the small building that was my home. I got up, loaded my musket, and prepared for battle. To my absolute surprise I saw that there was another man already inside my house. It was none other than Francois Pierre, who had been following the pirates as they tracked me across France.

"Well, in the end they were no match for us. I felt no remorse as we killed four of them, just as they would have killed me. The fifth managed to get away, and we were sure he would not try again now that the rest of his motley crew were dead.

"That was the second time Francois Pierre had saved my life.

"But that was not the end of it. The last man would not stop until he himself either died or exacted his terrible revenge. One day I felt his presence among the crowded streets and decided to head towards Italy, figuring that being a Frenchman, he would surely not want to follow. I was wrong.

"He caught up to me in Piedmont, where I fear I became careless. He shot me and left me for dead.

"And indeed, I thought that I had died. For when I awoke it was to the face of a beautiful angel standing over me. It was the person who turned out to be none other than your mother. I was injured badly, but she nursed me back to health over the course of the next two months. We grew close and I ended up working on the farm for her father, while she showed me the ways of God. We came to love each other and lay with each other one time.

"But her father, seeing that we had developed more than just a passing interest in each other, forbade any further contact and sent me away. She undoubtedly was already pregnant with you, although I had no knowledge of such developments.

"I had no choice but to return to France on this very same horse that is now pulling this cart. Old Luc. Who would have thought that this old nag would be the common thread that links the events of these two stories together. Anyway, I returned to work my land where I became a successful farmer. But I never stopped thinking about your mother and what might have been. That is a summary of my life that brings us to the present. And now I have a second chance with a son that I never knew I had."

Filipe has been quiet all this time. It's a lot for him to take in. He asks, "But if you loved my mother, why did you never return?"

"Ahhh, some things in life are not as easy as they may seem. I was a man trying to rebuild himself. Perhaps I did not think myself worthy. I was torn between my love for your mother and trying to respect the wishes of her father. And imagine if other pirates from the original crew had found me. What then? If I had known that you were already in your mother's belly my choices would have been very different. As it was, I believed that I was making the right decision for everyone."

*

* *

In time they arrive at their spiritual halfway point, the home of Francois Pierre. There is an odd eeriness about the place that had not been there before. The chickens are gone. Possibly eaten by foxes. Or stolen. It looks abandoned, which of course, is impossible.

Unless Francois were dead.

The thought creeps into Jean Pierre's mind like a cold wind. He tells Filipe to wait while he goes to reconnoitre the area. He finds Francois slumped at the little table where not so long ago the two of them drank rum and reminisced about a misspent life.

The fight had no doubt been fierce. Francois would not have gone easily. Jean wonders how many of the DuClerc rogues he had killed in his last stand. This is the third time the old pirate had saved his life. With a mixture of sadness and relief, Jean says his final goodbye to his old friend. "Well, old man, you got your wish. You died on your own terms. Sleep now, and we shall meet again on the great schooner in the sky."

Father and son prepare to bury their second body in as many weeks.

By the time they've seen to the dead body and cleaned up, the sun has all but disappeared behind the horizon. Jean Pierre grows anxious. "What is it father?" asks the boy.

"I cannot conceal the truth from you it seems. I am concerned that the men who killed Francois will return."

"I know how to handle a rifle if necessary. I nearly killed a man before."

"These are dangerous men with whom I have had run-ins before. You saw what they did to Francois. The real trick is knowing how to avoid a fight, to seek a peaceful outcome. This I learnt from none other than your mother. We will stay here and tonight, but we shall leave before sunrise."

Luc wakes Pierre up before sunrise with his characteristic whinnied warning. Adrenalin blows the cobwebs of tiredness away in an instant, and he silently goes to wake Filipe. He whispers to his son, "Shhh, we are not alone. Help me to stuff the beds with pillows and straw to make it look like we are still sleeping."

There's a ladder that reaches up into an attic of sorts that Francois once used for storage. Perhaps they can hide there unseen. Jean sends Filipe up first, passes their rifles up and climbs up after him. They wait among the dust and cobwebs in absolute stillness, like snow leopards waiting for their prey to pass underneath them.

Suddenly they hear footsteps from above. The would-be attackers are sneakier than first imagined. The roof creaks under the strain of a heavy body moving gingerly across the old tiles. Filipe waits, feeling the familiar weight of his grandfather's rifle in his hands. He looks at his father as if to whisper a question. Jean Pierre puts his finger to his lips and gestures towards the kitchen door.

Now the man above has stopped moving and there is a sound below. Someone is delicately trying the latch at the front door. The man who enters pauses and looks around, getting his bearings. Then he moves toward the two sleeping forms in the little bedroom off to the side of the kitchen area. Jean Pierre knows what's coming and indicates to Filipe that he should close his eyes. Two flashes illuminate the small house amidst the smoke and fiery thunder of gunfire as the man empties his muskets into the decoys.

The thug on the roof shouts, giving his position away, and Pierre shoots him instantly through the underside of the ceiling. The shot turns the clay tiles into deadly earthenware shrapnel that tears into the man's legs and testicles. He roars like a wounded bear and rolls off the roof, landing on the ground with wet thump.

Filipe opens his eyes and takes aim at the man below, who is still blinded from the flashes of his own muskets. He takes his time to make sure of his aim. His single shot rings out and in the aftermath of the explosion, Jean Pierre sees that the boy has caught the assailant squarely between the eyes. He's strangely impressed. The youngster is clearly his blood, and no mistaking.

The danger is not over yet though, and Jean Pierre again gestures to Filipe to keep silent. The man who fell off the roof is now calling for help from unseen associates.

They hear footsteps moving around the house from the rear. A voice tells his testicle-less comrade to keep quite while he tries to drag him away from further danger. Jean Pierre drops from his vantage point, quiet as a cat, and rolls out the front door, coming to a kneeling position with his rifle cocked against his shoulder in a firing position. The man stops and drops his wounded companion, looking defiantly at Jean Pierre. This is the second time the two men have faced each other in such circumstances.

DuClerc! Again.

Jean Pierre sees a movement out of the corner of his eye. A man has emerged from behind the wagon and is running directly at him. He swings the rifle towards the new assailant. He knows he has one chance to finish this. But he's done this before. The rifle is an extension of his arm and aiming is as intuitive as pointing a finger. The shot rings out and the ball finds its target in a bloody spray of bone and grey matter.

DuClerc has the distinct misfortune to see another of his brothers in crime dispatched by the same man. Jean Pierre spits on the ground in from of him and stares at the bandit ahead of him. He has shot his last bolt, and they both know has no more bullets without reloading. With that, the Swiss bandit is gone, back into the darkness whence he came.

Jean goes back to house to check on his son. The boy is sitting at the small table, rifle at the ready, but relaxes noticeably when he sees his father.

"Filipe, you are alive. Thank God. I'm sorry for this ungodly hell that follows me wherever I go. I've dragged you into something that I had hoped was at an end for me…"

The boy interrupts, "Father, I know you have done your best. Grandfather taught me that killing to save your own life is acceptable in the eyes of God. He would forgive us, for we should not be alive if we had not righteously protected each other."

Those who cook with love find their own happiness.

CHAPTER 10

Food and Peace

"Peace will come to the world when the people
have enough noodles to eat."
Momofuku Ando, father of instant noodles

The grandfather must have known Filipe would be a good hunter, perhaps recognising some of Filipe's wayward father in the boy. Now, years later, that same wayward father, who so desperately wants to create a life for the boy that is different from his own dark past, sees the same thing. Already there has been too much killing, and yet the boy seems oddly composed.

They begin to pack the wagon. One fills their water containers from the well while the other collects the hoard of dried sausages that have been maturing in the little kitchen. Since their arrival the day before, they have also accumulated quite an arsenal of weapons. Three rifles and four muskets from the dead bandits and another two, older, Italian matchlocks that the late ex-pirate had hidden in the same attic where Filipe and Jean Pierre had waited in ambush only hours earlier.

When they're ready to leave, they place the bodies inside the house and set fire to the structure. Neither bothers to look back as flames and sparks shoot heavenward.

Luc pulls them slowly along without protest. A very good sign, since the old beast's silence means the path is free of surprises. When they do make camp, they make sure to do so off the beaten track where they can hide the wagon in thick trees. Even so, Jean Pierre spends a good half an hour smoothing out the tracks and erasing as much sign of their passing as he can.

On these occasions, Filipe sets to work preparing food for the two of them. He skins, or plucks, whatever they've managed to hunt along the way. Then cooks the catch in one of the little pots that he has brought from his mother's house, together with wild mushrooms and various herbs and berries that he had either brought with him or gathered on the journey.

Sometimes he produces an aromatic tea made from nettles or green lemon balm, if they come across it along the way.

This evening the two of them sit together at dusk watching the sky turn from red to dark blue, as the approaching night air mingles with the scent of the approaching wintery air and the smell of food cooking over a small fire.

Filipe can't help but notice that the gruff demeanour that had adorned his father's face on that first encounter has been replaced by a smile. Perhaps it's the food, which Jean Pierre confesses he does not believe comes from such a simple kitchen. He tells his son that he cooks like only one other person, and that the boy has surely inherited his mother's culinary gifts.

The boy agrees that he learned to cook from his mother, and that it is something that he very much likes to do. "Mother always said heart and soul were the most important ingredients to any dish, and those who cook with love find their own happiness in the journey."

"Indeed? I think you are very much your mother's son."

Filipe, enjoying the attention he's getting from his father, adds, "And grandfather always said that we were at peace after a good meal."

But by this time Jean Pierre is too engrossed in the deliciousness of his meal to respond.

They both eat in silence for a while.

Jean Pierre sneaks a glance at the boy who seems to come out of his shell whenever the subject of food and cooking comes up. "Son, I will tell you a story…

"A long time ago, I was on a ship off the coast of Peru. Well, we were floundering, having taken some damage from a collision with another vessel, so we decided to put ashore to make repairs.

"We encountered a group of Inca Indians, and after some negotiation with the help of a man who had some experience with the local language and culture, we managed to come to an understanding between us. They supplied us with the wood we needed to repair the ship, and in exchange, we gave them two guns plus enough ammunition for a small ambush, as well as some knives, rum, and mirrors.

"When all was said and done, we were happy with the materials we'd been able to procure, and they were more than happy with the goods that they had managed to get from us. Especially the rum. It was the beginning of a great friendship between pirates and native people. Through another extended series of gestures and verbalisations, we realised that we had been invited to their small village where we were to be treated to a feast.

"Presently we found ourselves above the river valley on a large rocky shelf that was big enough to serve as a permanent encampment for the tribe. At one end, skins had been stitched together with leather strops and strung from a rocky overhang for cover. There was a communal area where logs had been arranged to form seating and were covered with animal hides.

"The shelf itself backed into a large cave-like opening which clearly served as a primitive kitchen. Huge clay pots, the size of a stooped man, stood in a circle around a fire pit at one side. There were wooden frames made from tree-branches, from which hung herbs, peppers and other edible plants, dried fish, and various pieces of cooking paraphernalia.

"Whatever we may have thought about these primitive natives previously, the advanced organisation of their encampment gave us a new perspective.

"We sat at the far side of the entrance, away from the smoke of the fire, on rugs made from grasses and embellished with small mottled green stones. We drank rum and conversed as best we could, but really, we only managed to compare weaponry; their spears and our cutlasses; we gave a small demonstration of how to load the flintlocks we had given them.

"After a while, a man who we had not seen before arrived among us. We thought that he must be some kind of shaman, or headman, by the way he was dressed and way the other natives treated him. Again, through our limited interpretation abilities, we were able to understand that he was welcoming us as guests on behalf of the whole tribe, telling us that they were preparing a special feast for us the following day, and that we should remain here with them until that time.

"The environment was pleasant enough, so, having nothing better to do other than the arduous task of repairing the ship, we agreed, and sent men to collect more rum from the ship.

"The next morning, we awoke to find preparations in full swing. It was clear that we were expected to join in.

"The centrepiece of the meal was to be some kind of local wild-pig, they used the word peccary to describe it, stuffed with various herbs and vegetables."

Jean Pierre notices that Filipe's eyes have widened with interest, and he is listening intently. The boy has even taken out a notebook and a small pencil to make notes on the exotic recipe.

"Well, peccaries existed in abundance in the nearby forests and are like small, less dangerous versions of the wild boars we have in France. A hunting party had brought back six of these, which they had cleaned – away from the encampment for reasons of hygiene – and then skinned with the guts removed for crab bait.

"Like wild boar, the meat of the peccary is very lean and can be tough if not prepared correctly. But the Indians had a very special method of making the meat soft, which involved inserting coca leaves between the joints and sinews. They explained that the coca released an enzyme when cooked that softened down sinews and tenderized the meat. We had been hearing stories about these leaves for some time from the Spanish in the area who said that they could be chewed to produce a light stimulant effect.

"Despite our ship's cook being the only one among us even vaguely familiar with the procedures of cooking, we all set about the preparations enthusiastically, under the watchful eye of several women who oversaw the kitchen operations.

"Our first job was to pierce the outer skin of the animals with thin sharp knives, much like the one I have seen you using when you dress your prey. This was done so that slivers of wild duck fat could be inserted between the skin and the body of the wild pork. Our hosts explained that this helped to keep the meat from drying out over the long cooking time of several hours.

"We made a paste from sea-salt and green garlic and rubbed this liberally on the outside of the skin. Some of the women stuffed whole sprigs of various herbs into the breast cavities against the inside of the ribs of the small animals.

"When all this was done, the meat was wrapped in banana leaves, along with yams, potatoes, hot peppers, onions, wild leeks, and an aromatic herb, perhaps a bit like your Italian arugula, which they called *quirquiña*, and placed into the clay pots.

"Now the real cooking could begin. The pots were lowered into the fire pit and positioned some distance above the flames. A special type of aromatic wood had been used, which, according to our hosts was important for the flavour of the food. After about two hours, when the once enormous flames had died down, the clay pots were lowered further, bringing them into contact with the embers and red-hot coals at the bottom of the pit.

"The Indians covered the pots with earth, and there we left them for several hours.

"While the main feast slowly cooked in the underground ovens, we drank liquor made from manioc and ate dishes made of corn and cassava with a spicy soup to wash them down.

"Later, women in festive costumes joined us and offered us small bitter pieces of dried plants to eat, which had a pleasantly intoxicating effect. The mood became lighter and lighter, and we got swept up in it, dancing and chanting until it seemed we had all become part of some collective frenzied ritual.

"The dimensions of the rock encampment shifted and changed under the influence of the strange plant, and time seemed to race ahead and stand still at the same time, until suddenly the food was ready. As they pulled the clay pots from the ground and opened them up, the food released a fragrance that not only smelled incredible, but elicited visions of colour as it interacted with our senses."

Jena Pierre seems to be caught up in the moment of remembering the experience. "I can say with confidence that this was undoubtedly the most delicious meal I have ever eaten. And in the days following the feast, everything seemed brighter and more colourful. We also found that the coca leaves gave us a newfound energy for undertaking the repairs to the ship."

Jean Pierre is quite animated now, "By the gods, I wager your mother would have enjoyed that meal," and then he looks at Filipe, "perhaps one day you will find your own shaman to cook with."

They both laugh at the story.

And then Filipe says something that would come to define his later purpose in life, even though he could not possibly have known it then. "Isn't it amazing that despite having great cultural differences, it was food that brought your pirate crew together with the Indian tribe. No fighting, just a common enjoyment of food. Food and peace.

"How lucky you are to have had such experiences from travels. It's a dream of mine to also travel the world and learn about the different kinds of food. Please tell me more about your adventures if you are so inclined."

This takes Jean Pierre completely by surprise. How grown up this boy is for his age. He certainly had not thought himself lucky. But to a boy who had lost his mother so recently, perhaps lucky was a relative term. And in a strange and terrible kind of way, the boy's bad luck had turned out to be his own good luck.

"Perhaps we are both lucky to have found each other," says Jean Pierre.

By now the sun has disappeared below the horizon, and both are fatigued from travelling. They fall fitfully asleep next to the small fire, with their rifles not far away.

*

* *

In the weeks that follow they cover the many miles back to Jean Pierre's home in similar fashion, travelling by day, getting to know each other over a small fire and a big-hearted meal. When they finally arrive back at the homestead, the drunken caretaker is miraculously no longer drunk.

Pierre thinks to himself that the rogue must have run out of drink, or money to buy drink, or both. Or maybe Laetitia's spirit has travelled with them and blessed them all. It never occurs to him that his own grumpiness might have been at least in some part responsible for the man's unhappiness.

He introduces the new young master of the farm to the caretaker. Piotr is his name, meaning "Rock," being from good Polish Catholic descent. Piotr welcomes them happily and smiles broadly, thinking now that Pierre has a son to talk to, he might be less grumpy.

Happy reunions over and done with, Jean Pierre takes his son inside the house to show him his new home. Meanwhile Piotr attends to the old horse, who just might be the real hero of this adventure. He brings him carrots and sugar lumps, and washes the salt off the old beast's neck, gives him a good old brush, and leads him into the pasture behind the house.

Jean Pierre, perhaps feeling guilty about not attending to the horse as is his usual practice, comes out briefly to check on him. But, Luc, being a horse, is thinking only horsey thoughts and is happily munching on a hay bale.

Son and father each miss Laetitia in their own way. Everything is new to Filipe, and he undoubtedly needs time to figure it out for himself. Jean Pierre is happy that he finally has his own flesh and blood near to him. A new family unit is forming.

That night, Jean Pierre, Piotr and Filipe dine on roast chicken and vegetables from the gardens of Filipe's new home. And they toast to the beginning of a new era.

*

* *

The three of them begin to settle into a routine that involves doing whatever working the farm involves. Early mornings and heavy work leave them tired to the point of exhaustion at the end of each long day. Filipe and his father often go to bed early, glad that the daily toil means sleep come easily, even if that sleep sometimes brings with it unfriendly dreams.

But something in particular still bothers Jean Pierre, and he resolves to have it out. On a quiet, cool, clear-skied morning, Jean Pierre speaks of his concerns to Filipe and Piotr over a breakfast of cornbread and strong tea.

"I fear we have not seen the last of the men who killed Francois and tried to ambush us. I have been lucky enough to come away from my encounters with them with my skin intact on two occasions. And on both occasions, they have gone away with fewer men than they started with. Revenge is a religious compulsion with these people. And we are their devil."

He notices Piotr's anxious demeanour at hearing the story and tries to allay his fears. "I cannot say for sure that they will follow us here. But perhaps we should at least strategise against that eventuality."

Within the hour, the three have agreed on a course of action. They will build a series of surprises and traps around the property that at the very least might give them warning of any encroaching danger. Holes in the ground will be dug in strategic places, with sharpened wooden stakes placed at the bottom, and the openings concealed with small branches and grass. They will hide caches of weapons and ammunition at tactically advantageous points for easy access. They will create a lookout point in the high boughs of the nearby fig tree. And they will secret pistols and muskets within reach in the frequently used locales such as the stables and outhouses.

Jean Pierre's concerns are unfounded, however, and the weeks became months, until more than a year has passed. They make great progress in renovating and improving the workings of the farm. New fields are dug. Special oxides are applied to the barn to give the wood colour. Slowly but surely, gratifying reforms create a new kingdom in a place that was previously neglected.

Even Piotr has made an effort to swear off the alcohol, at least while working. No one resents him the small beer he has with his breakfast, or the glass of wine with dinner. The sober life agrees with him as much as it agrees with everyone around him, and soon he finds himself a girlfriend, Mary. One thing leads to another, as these things usually do, and in good time they are joined in matrimony at a simple yet charming little wedding. Jean Pierre is honoured to serve as ring bearer. Filipe cooks up a feast with the help of the neighbours.

Following the wedding, Mary comes to work on the farm alongside Filipe in the kitchen. They make a formidable team, cooking for the growing family, and reinforcing Filipe's belief in the power of good food to create harmony and happiness.

Aftermath of the battle in Paris.

CHAPTER 11

Pot au feu

"If more of us valued food and cheer and song
above hoarded gold, it would be a merrier world."
The Hobbit by J.R.R Tolkien

On a June day in 1789, Jean Pierre and Filipe are
readying a cartload of early season potatoes for transport to
market. These are a style favoured by the discerning appetites
of Parisian restaurateurs, nobles and bourgeoisie alike, and
the two gentlemen farmers are confident that their crop will
bring a healthy profit. To help matters along, as is their
typical practice, Jean Pierre and Filipe have washed the crop
in the nearby stream, adding to their appeal.

The pair take to the road happily, Jean Pierre humming
lively Parisian tunes and Filipe talking excitedly about recipes
and what spices from India and North Africa he might find
at the markets in exchange for some of their crop.

Old Luc picks his way carefully along a cobbled path
that's been worn smooth from thousands of years of Roman
traffic and made slippery in places by the previous night's
rain that has yet to evaporate in the early morning sun.

Arriving among the bustle and smells of the markets on the outskirts of Paris, it doesn't take the trio long to empty their cart, save for a special consignment designated for a special customer near the Port of Paris, the tavern and lodging of one Rebecca Poitier.

This last stop is no ordinary delivery of simple tubers, however, washed or otherwise. Filipe realises that his father and this woman are friends. There is an unpretentious atmosphere of affection between the two of them, but not in a way that threatens Filipe. She's a genuinely likeable person. "What a handsome young man your son is." Filipe feels his cheeks growing red. "He's a good influence on you, Jean, you look years younger. I know what it is; you're smiling more.

"Why don't the two of you stay here for the night. I'm making my famous pot-au-feu with marrowbone, and these lovely potatoes you have brought me will make a welcome addition. We'll have a little wine and cheese. I'm sure you and I can think of a few ways to entertain ourselves," she winks at him, "why rush back? No doubt Filipe could do with a change of scenery from the farm."

Jean Pierre hesitates a moment. The offer is tempting. Rebecca's pot au feu is a legend in its own dinnertime. "Thank you, Rebecca, but I don't like leaving Piotr and Maria alone for too long. I think we'll go back today. We will share a glass with you before we go, though."

"So you shall. And I'll give you some fresh garlic bread for the journey home. You and Filipe are always welcome, as I am sure you know."

*

* *

As they set out on the journey back home, Pierre smiles at Filipe, showing him the bag of coins that represents the day's takings. Filipe grins back almost involuntarily. His father's jubilant mood is infectious, and the two of them are leaving the capital in high spirits. Their wares are always a hit among customers appreciative of quality produce.

Luc, needing no guidance other than his own innate sense of direction, plods back along the well-worn path, towing the now much lighter cart along with a deceptive ease for such an old animal. Perhaps his advanced age has rendered him a bit deaf, because the old beast fails to realise the danger that follows them. There's no customary whinny from the horse when Jean Pierre's nemesis, the elder DuClerc, and two others, creep along several cart lengths behind, observing their progress unseen. The deaths of Jean Pierre and Filipe would be sweet enough, but here was also the added bonus of the bag of coin they were carrying, too.

The thugs have been following them for about two miles, wating for a place where there will be the fewest witnesses. Now they see their chance. The cart will have to pass through a short tunnel that leads through the old city walls, forming a dark choke point, difficult to get out of, once in.

As they enter the tunnel, something seems to bother Luc. The horse makes no sound, but tries to turn his head backward, confounding the reigns somewhat. Perhaps this, along with the fact that his eyes need to adjust to the

105

darkness inside the tunnel, and the slippery, rocky incline at the ingress to the portal, cause the animal to move more trepidatiously than normal. The dark liminal space of the tunnel entrance is enough to create the opportunity the bandits have been waiting for.

Just as Filipe's eyes are becoming accustomed to the dimness, he glimpses a movement in front of Luc. Luc bucks and snorts three times and stops short. Jean Pierre leans back and somersaults lithely into the back of the cart. He may be a gentleman farmer now, but he still has the reflexes of a pirate.

A shot rings out and Filipe, who has already jumped down and is holding Luc's reigns to stop the animal injuring himself, reflexively looks toward his father, now standing in the cart, clutching at his chest. In slow motion, blood is forming a bright red rosette in the fabric of his shirt. Jean Pierre crumples over the side of the cart, still holding his rifle in his hand, a perplexed look on his face.

The man responsible for the shot is standing in a cloud of smoke about a meter or so forward and to the right of Luc. He drops his weapon and fumbles for a second one in his waistband. The commotion has spooked Luc, who rears up on his hind legs, pulling the reigns from Filipe's grip, and knocking him to the ground.

The shooter barely manages to get his hands on his other gun before Luc's hooves find the top of his skull. With an odd squelching sound, the man's head disintegrates, flinging pieces of bone and what little brains he has in all directions.

Filipe, still on the ground can see bits of hair stuck in Luc's horseshoes. The moment of confusion gives him the split second he needs. In one elastic movement he wrenches the rifle from his father's cold dead hands, rolls to the side, aims and fires at another of the atrocious worms who has stationed himself behind the cart.

No sooner has the ball from Filipe's rifle found its mark between the eyes of the second thug, than a third shot rings out. This time, a musket ball takes the top of Filipe's ear with it. Filipe, not wanting to remain a target, rolls again and springs like a dangerous monkey up and over the side of the cart to where his rifle lies, loaded and unused.

DuClerc the elder is fumbling with his rifle, perfectly silhouetted against the brightness of the tunnel entrance. It's an easy shot for Filipe the hunter, and the lead ball strikes the patriarch of this evil posse that has pursued them for two years smack bang in the middle of his chest.

The force of the shot knocks DuClerc onto his backside. As he falls, he emits a howl like demons being exorcised from his blackened soul. Filipe is upon him, stabbing him in the neck with his armadillo-tail-handled skinning knife. With his last breath the bandit gurgles a final curse, "Blast you and your kind. I have spent a great deal of time and energy hounding the killer of my sons. Now you have killed us all. I condemn you to a hell worse than mine." And with that he dies in a pool of his own sticky black blood.

Filipe quickly scans the tunnel for further signs of danger. Seeing none, he approaches his father to check on his injuries. It doesn't look good. Jean Pierre, lover, father, and pirate, has fought his last battle. When he speaks, his voice is as soft as a whisper, "I'm sorry to have dragged you into this my son. Would that it had been otherwise. Keep your distance from this place and avoid these rogues. They are hell bent on seeing us dead..."

Through tears, the boy interrupts him and places an arm under him as though trying to pick him up. "Come father, we must get you to a doctor."

Jean Pierre musters the last of his strength and pulls the boy's arm away. "No doctor can save me now. Stay with me for a moment." He pulls the bag of the day's coin from inside his coat. "It was a good day, was it not, Filipe?" The smile on his face as he talks to his son at that moment is one that Filipe will never forget. It's almost serene. "All I ever wanted was to have you by my side. I am thankful that God gave me that opportunity. Perhaps He will forgive me the great debt I owe heaven. Just as He has given me the chance to die in the arms of my only son."

His breathing gets shallower, and his voice grows more urgent, "You are a man now. Go to Rebecca's boarding house and remain there until the coast is clear." The effort of speaking is too much, and he coughs up more blood, "ahh…I will go now to join your mother, my great love. The life with her that I missed in this world, I shall have somewhere out of it."

He dies with a smile on his face.

It's a strange sensation for Filipe, to lose a father he had only known for such a short period of time. He does not understand the anger of men. He hopes his father will find peace in the next world. He stands up and looks around. The battle has consumed them all. Even the horse, old Luc, is dead. Perhaps he died in sympathy with his owner.

Curiously, the leaves on the trees at the entrance of the tunnel begin to rustle. A gust of wind mysteriously materialises, as though to collect the souls of Jean Pierre and his trusty steed, Luc, and transport them through the portal to the other side.

Filipe didn't get a chance to tell his father that the bandits were all dead. Nonetheless, he will heed his father's final words. One never knew what other rogues might want to claim revenge on their behalf.

Death follows after Filipe.

CHAPTER 12

Out of the frying pan

"There's no shame in fear, my father told me,
what matters is how we face it."
A Clash of Kings, by George R.R. Martin

The clatter of gunfire has drawn a crowd of nosey parkers. Inquisitive onlookers, raggedy travellers, market-stall owners with too few customers, idlers with too much time and other wasters who can't contain their curiosity jostle for a better glimpse of what has transpired in the dim tunnel.

A whistle shrieks, followed by the sound of heavy boots accompanied by wheezing. The crowd opens up like the Red Sea parting in order to allow a panting, enormously fat, lawman to pass. The pot-bellied policeman still has pieces of his lunch stuck in his moustache and smeared on the front of his tunic. Whatever he was eating, he must have been shovelling it in with gusto. By the look on his face, it's clearly a huge annoyance that he's been interrupted, gunfire or not.

The effort of getting to the scene of the crime has left him breathless. He stands with his hand on his chest, chuffing like a steam-train. Once he's able to breathe again, he surveys the carnage. Three dead bandits, one with a crushed skull, a fourth dead man, a boy, bent over the latter crying, and a horse, also dead. Not your everyday traffic jam.

The fat policeman surmises, correctly, that the body of Jean Pierre is the victim of a robbery gone wrong, and the boy must be his son. Whatever else we may think of this overweight officer, we must not make the mistake of thinking that he can't do his job. He bends down to speak to the boy in a soft, sympathetic tone.

Filipe doesn't want to leave his father, but the policeman gently coaxes the boy into letting go of the body and moves him to a place closer to the entrance to the tunnel. Now, in better light, the policeman sees that Filipe is in shock. The poor boy's face is pale, and his lips are trembling. Words come tumbling out of his mouth, something about bandits and revenge and potatoes and coin.

The policeman doesn't know quite what to make of potatoes in the context of the bloodshed before him, but he certainly understands bandits. He shrugs, "There are many bandits in Paris on hot days like this. They slip the gates of hell and find sport here."

He also understands coin, and his ministrations towards the boy take on a more mercenary tone. "Of course, we will have to see to the dead bodies. Better to take care of it now before the magistrates get involved."

In his bewildered state Filipe agrees to whatever the man suggests, and soon more men arrive in two carts. In one cart they place the four dead bodies, and in the other, the horse, along with the broken pieces of what remains of Jean Pierre's cart.

Soon Filipe finds himself part of an impromptu funeral procession that looks more like some kind of black circus than anything else. The carts reach the back of a small graveyard. It can hardly be called a cemetery. There are no proper gravestones. The grass is long and weeds grow everywhere. There is a fetid ditch to one side into which they unceremoniously throw the three bandits. The matter of the boy's father is a little more delicate.

They take Jean Pierre's body to a separate part of the small plot where a small grove of scraggly trees struggles to suck enough nutrients from the depleted soil. A proper grave has been dug here, if one can call it that.

The gravedigger stands with his head bowed as Jean Pierre's body is deposited into the hole, only somewhat more carefully than how the bandits were handled. As Filipe watches on, he feels a presence at his side. A priest has mysteriously also materialised at the graveside.

He prays for Jean Pierre's soul in a clear, beautiful voice, his words like birds taking flight as though startled amidst the scrub and unkempt chaos of the graveyard.

Eulogy over, he too, extracts his price from Filipe, caring more for his own purse than for the souls buried there, and disappears as mysteriously as he had appeared, leaving the boy alone with the gravedigger.

"Boy, is that animal in the cart over there yours?" Filipe wonders what he's getting at, and how much more of his money he'll be wanting.

"Yes… well…no. It was my father's horse. His name was Luc. I guess in a strange way they were friends, if there can really be a friendship between man and animal."

The gravedigger eyes the boy from under the brim of his flea-bitten hat, "Well, I don't mean to offend your young lordship…" here Filipe can't tell if he's being sarcastic or not, "but if you allow me, for some of that coin, I would be happy to bury the beast alongside your father. To ease his passage in the next life, you understand."

What little Filipe understands about the murky and opaque workings of the church, he's pretty sure what the gravedigger is suggesting is forbidden. Certainly his mother, a fervent catholic would have been horrified at the mere suggestion of such a thing. But the idea fascinates his young, curious mind. His father would probably like having Luc buy his side, after all, the kings and knights of olden times practiced this ritual.

The gravedigger intuits what running through the boy's mind, "Heed not the superstitions of the priests boy. They see not what I see in this unfortunate place. It is good that we do not separate them. Your father will be needing a strong animal to carry him across the Styx. They shall both go to a better place together."

He hands over the price the gravedigger asks, which is more than half of what he has left, and helps the man lower the beast into the hole on top of Jean Pierre's body.

With nothing left to do, Filipe watches the man shovel soil over his father and what's left of Luc, then turns his back and sets off for Rebecca's place.

*

* *

Twilight comes, as it inevitably must, bringing with it the lamplighters with their long poles and wicks to light the whale-oil lamps that illuminate the streets of modern cities such as this. The fuel gives off a faint fishy aroma as it burns, but the crude light improves the way, and its smell is the least of the odours permeating the streets of the old city.

For some reason Filipe wanders off the main street. No-one can blame him for being more than a little distracted by the events of the day. In the shadows of this side street two street urchins, around eight or nine years old, appear in front of him. He laments the fact that his armaments had been confiscated earlier by the fat policeman. But by the sight of their badly-home-made weapons he calculates these boys are ill-prepared for what might potentially follow.

"Brats. Know that I am too tired to trifle with you. I should kill you both, just as I dispatched two bandits near the city gate today. But I have had enough of death. Instead, I shall give you a little coin, so that you might dwell on the notion of human gratitude, and perhaps reform your ways before someone less merciful does kill you."

He digs two coins out of his remaining stash and hands them over. Then he turns his back on them without any concern that they might attack and continues on to Rebecca's boarding house.

115

Rebecca is beside herself once Filipe recounts his story of the day's unpleasantnesses. She makes no attempt to hide the salty tears that run down her face. The woman had known Jean Pierre for many years and her loss is palpable. She puts her arms around Filipe, as much to console herself as him. "You must stay here, as long as you need."

Filipe wants to try to pay for the room. He's only got four coins left in the blood-stained bag, which he hands over to her. Some debate ensues; she neither needs nor wants any money from him, after all he's the son of a dear friend, and besides, any bill has surely been paid many times over with France's most beautiful potatoes. Ultimately, she holds onto the bag with the intention of keeping it safe for the boy until he needs it.

She offers Filipe some tea and sits with him while he drinks. When he's done, she motions to the stairs and shows him to one of the rooms upstairs. There's a basin, which she fills with warm water from the stove, and a half bar of soap. She asks for the boy's clothes for the washerwoman and produces a clean set that had belonged to one of the guests. A little big, but they'll do.

A million thoughts cascade though Filipe's mind as he sits on the bed, none of them very coherent. Head and stomach are churning, and he can't bring himself to eat the meal of chicken soup with garlic and bread. At some point he falls asleep, and the horrors of the day follow him into the land of nightmares.

By morning he's unable to tell if he's slept or not, unable to separate dream from reality. The ordeal has left him groggy. Perhaps he's still dreaming. No, he can't be. He's sitting on the side of the bed, head in his hands, with his toes just touching the ground. Not quite of Rodin's Thinker, though it could be argued that the boy has indeed seen the gates of Hell. I know life's not supposed to be easy, he thinks to himself. But if only it were less cruel.

He drags himself to the Louis XV washbasin. The water from last night is cold now, but the shock of it feels real on his face. It's as though he's washing the messiness of the dream-world away.

At the same time, he hears a great commotion coming from the street. Could this be the start of the revolution everyone's been whispering about?

Filipe meets chef Francesc and Tereza.

CHAPTER 13

Jam side down

"Everywhere I hear the sound of marchin',
chargin' feet, boy 'cause summer's here and the
time is right for fighting in the street, boy"
Rolling Stones, Street Fighting Man

The sound of explosions would be remembered as a black mark on that fine summer day. The neighbourhood around Rebecca's boarding house reverberates as gunpowder kegs are detonated and black sulphurous clouds billow skyward. The smell of smoke is everywhere. The once whispered voice of the revolution is growing into a shout, louder and more insistent.

Hunger and disenchantment were no strangers to the other great European capitals, but Paris for its own reasons had become the epicentre of discontent. Ordinary people had grown tired of the excesses of the royalty and the wasteful hedonism of the bourgeoisie. Clandestine pamphlets condemning the immorality of the queen have been circulating in intellectual circles. For some time now, the newspapers have been carrying themes that challenge traditional societal structures and dogmas.

Looking through the window, Felipe sees soldiers looking on wearily while men and women run with shovels that only weeks hence will become weapons, along with the pitchforks and hoes that once were nothing more than farming tools. But for now, the shovels are for putting out fires and moving rubble.

He runs down the stairs intending to join the throng. He needs to get outside. To occupy himself. To forget his own sorry state of being. Rebecca heads him off before he can reach the door. "Filipe, you must stay here. A revolution is nigh, and you cannot risk being among the crowd if the fighting starts."

"But we have to do something."

"Look at me Filipe and trust my words. Your father, bless his soul, would never forgive me if anything happened to you. This is not the time for a boy to be outside. Only last week fighting broke out when the army tried to round up the young men and make them enlist. And today, houses are being burnt. No. Too much misfortune has already befallen your young life. I implore you, remain here where you can be safe."

At the mention of his father, Filipe reluctantly agrees. Perhaps he will stay here and look after Rebecca.

Just then he becomes aware of another pair of eyes watching him. Rebecca's six-year-old daughter, Ana, has been inquisitively observing him from behind a counter in the foyer. He knows who she is from previous potato deliveries. She smiles at him with an unabashed smile, her slightly dirty little face a picture of innocence.

It's a long time since Filipe has seen such a picture of unaffected sincerity. Her beautiful smile is reminiscent of a baroque painting, a lightness contrasted against the dark mood of their current situation.

She speaks, affecting the serious tone that only young children can. It was a sentence that Filipe would never forget, even though at the time it seemed rather more funny than serious. "Monsieur Felipe, when I grow up, I'm going to marry you."

Then she darts away, leaving Filipe with a bemused smile. And at that moment he forgets about the misfortunes of the past day, the chaos of the world outside. It's a good moment. One that he will carry with him.

*

* *

Another hot night passes without any wind to blow the city clean. When Filipe wakes up the next morning, the sun is already beating down on the capital. The atmosphere in the tavern is stifling, so he decides to venture out into the streets. Up on Montmartre, soldiers are kicking up dust, while down here in the little cobbled streets, citizens go about their chaotic business like ants raiding a rival's colony. He sees queues of people lining up for a hot meal, haggling for old clothing, or arguing with each other about politics.

As he wanders the streets, avoiding the puddles from last night's chamber pots, he realises that he does not like Paris. Too grimy. Too much confusion. Too much noise.

Too many people. He misses the quiet peacefulness of the farm where he and his father had lived until two days ago. But he cannot go back. Not yet. His father's last words still ring in his mind.

With all these thoughts bumping around in his head he realises that he has no idea where he is. Looking around, he finds himself in a small street that's unlike the dirty chaos he's just left behind. Here the shopfronts are decidedly fancier. Among the cascades of flowers in various planters he sees a mosaiced sign that reads Restaurant Petit.

Restaurant is not a word Filipe is familiar with, but curiosity draws him toward the window. Looking inside he sees some small chairs and tables with blue and white cloths draped over them. Behind those he sees two baskets of bread atop a small counter.

A bakery thinks Filipe to himself, or even a tavern. But why so fancy? This is nothing like even the Paris bouillons that he has helped his father deliver potatoes to.

But there is something else that catches his eye. Right alongside the baskets, stacked on silver serving platters, he sees multi-layered galettes, sugary brioches and other puffed-up pastries, some with brightly coloured confitures that remind him of the preserved fruit his mother used to make, only these look more refined. The food is covered with a delicate, almost transparent cloth that gives it a noble complexion.

Leaving aside the very real fact that he hasn't eaten properly since his father was murdered by highwaymen, this is nothing short of a miracle for a boy of Filipe's imagination and inclination.

He presses his face to window to get a better view of the culinary cornucopia within. It's not only bread and cakes that make up this gastronomical *mise-en-scène*. There's an entire section devoted to cheeses and cured meats. Filipe recognises the salamis, sausages and whole legs of ham from the farm in France as well as back in Italy. But there are also many special cuts that he is not familiar with. As with the pastries, these, too, are covered in the delicate transparent cloth, tied with golden lace bows.

The world that the young man has inhabited until only a short time ago is totally forgotten. Young Filipe is completely mesmerised by what he is seeing. It never occurred to him that food and cooking could be anything but sustenance. Sure, he himself liked to experiment with flavours and preparations, and invent new dishes. But here was not just cooking, this was something more like art.

At this point he has climbed onto a small flowerpot and is leaning against the window with hands cupped into the shape of an imaginary viewing glass to block out some of the glare coming from the sunlit street. The rickety, eroded wood of the shopwindow frame, that until now has been the only thing between him and the fantastical culinary charms within, gives way in a noisy clatter of glass and splinters.

Filipe tumbles in and rolls under a table stacked with cakes and other delights. The stunned boy sits up, only to knock his head on the underside the table. This causes him to involuntarily fall back to the floor, whereupon the entire arrangement comes tumbling down around him and deposits a particularly sticky pastry, jam side down, onto his face.

If the situation were not so risky it might have been funny. He staggers to his feet and thinks of trying to pick up the cakes before anyone finds him, but of course that's impossible. He's covered in cream and red confiture that makes him look like a mock victim in one of those silly slapstick plays, put on by wandering players, involving kicks to the backside and pies to the face.

Before he can escape, a girl in a white apron appears. "*Merde!* Who are you? What nonsense is zis? If you are the new kitchen boy we have been expecting, you're not off to a very good start. Look what you have done. Chef Petit will eat you alive. Perhaps it is better you run away before he gets his hands and teeth on you."

Filipe has a vision of a giant man with hairy ears and crooked teeth. The voice that calls after the girl is nothing like Filipe imagines a giant's voice to sound. "Mon Dieu. Are we finally at war with the English?" The voice is that of an educated man. A little effete, perhaps, but that could be due to the peevish tone of someone in a high state of irritation at having his carefully curated domain disrupted.

The owner of the voice appears at the stairs, pastry knife in hand, and glares at the boy standing amidst the destruction. "Is this the kitchen boy I was expecting a week ago? This will never do. Not only are you late, but destroying my creations not five minutes after setting foot in my restaurant shows a considerable audacity *n'est-ce pas?*"

The jig is well and truly up. With nowhere to run, Filipe must now face his accuser. He raises his eyes bashfully and sees an elegant Frenchman in crisp chef's whites. The man is tall and thin with elegant, slender fingers ideal for the delicate work involved in creating his art. He regards Filipe with piercing azure eyes that look out over a Gallic nose, eyebrows arched enquiringly. "Speak, boy."

Filipe summons all the courage he can muster, "please sir, I was just admiring your beautiful cakes. I have never seen anything like it before. The window…I never meant to…I mean it broke and I fell into your shop. I'm sorry, your creations…it was an accident…"

The chef cuts him short, "An accident? An accident? Mince! There are no accidents, there is only clumsiness. Do you know what you have done? Where you see merely beautiful cakes, I see art! But this is not even the worst of it. The cakes, they are easy to replace, but you have destroyed something ir-re-place-able." He says this last word with extra emphasis and glares down at Filipe.

"You have torn my precious cloth, my Dhaka Muslin. Do you know what that is? I suppose not. This is a fabric so rare it is impossible to obtain, even on the black-markets. So rare that Marie Antoinette herself is said to have bought the last remaining bolt from a travelling trader who found it along the Silk Road. No, this is more than just a fabric. It's worth cannot be measured. Some say it is woven from the skin of the moon, or from the very air around us by magician-weavers. And that is why it is the only thing to protect my creations from attack by flying pests. *Bof* !, apparently it cannot protect against all flying pests."

But Filipe is no ordinary boy, as the man called Francesc Alain Petit is about to discover. His response takes the great chef by surprise.

"I am very sorry about ruining your cloth, for I have seen its kind before."

The chef's eyebrows climb higher on his head like two animated caterpillars, and he lets out an astonished laugh.

"No, it's true. My grandfather had some amongst his treasures before he died. He sold it to a dressmaker from Milano who made clothing for the noble women. The money he received was enough to pay for the farm's expenses for some years."

"A pretty story. But hard to believe."

Greatly relieved that he hasn't been eaten alive and determined to find some common ground with the man responsible for all these creations, Filipe continues to tell the story of how his grandfather had come into possession of that rarest of fabrics.

On a day sometime in the past an oriental traveller had appeared on his grandfather's farm. The man had been attacked by unknown assailants, who tried to rob him, and had been badly wounded in the fracas that ensued as he fought them off. The grandfather, being a good Christian soul, naturally offered him shelter.

The man mended slowly and struck up a friendship with the grandfather. The two men discovered that that they had much in common. Like the grandfather, the traveller, too, was a devout man, but took his learnings from the Qur'an. The two old gentlemen would sit and debate the meaning of

God and life for hours on end, each paying special care to respect the other's point of view.

When Filipe asked his grandfather why he was so tolerant, the grandfather smiled and told him that no matter what name men gave Him, the teachings of God were one and the same for all religions. What really mattered, he said, was honour and respect for one's fellows.

When the time came for the man to continue his journey, the oriental traveller revealed the treasure he'd fought so hard to protect from the bandits. It was none other than the same precious cloth that Filipe had seen here today.

"I remember because my grandfather also called it the Fabric of Dhaka, one of the cities on the famous Silk Road. Well, as I said, he sold it to a Milanese, who claimed it was the most valuable thing he had ever seen. He told that story whenever he could, and the cloth became a sort of legend because no one had ever seen anything like it before or after. Until today. You have the same cloth as my grandfather had."

The chef just stands and looks at Filipe. If nothing else, the boy has a vivid imagination. Whether real or not, the story reveals a quick mind.

"Per'aps zere is more in common zan I imagined," he declares in his precise French way. "Bon. You are hired. But I will take fifteen days wages for the destruction.

"Now, let us review the letter of approval from your father for your apprenticeship, empowering me with your education and instruction here in what I like to call my emporium of delicacies. Héhéhé" He's clearly amused at his own description, imagining the words in the mouths of his customers.

Filipe has an idea of what has happened here – the chef has clearly mistaken him for someone else. The girl from before had referred to him as the new kitchen boy. He feels like there's enough trouble and confusion here without piling a lie on top of everything else.

"Sir…," he starts.

"The only sir I know is a sirloin. I am the great chef Francesc Alain Petit. To you I am simply Chef, or if you will, Chef Francesc."

"Yes sir…I mean Chef. I would love with all my heart to stay here, but I am not the boy whose father sent you the letter. That boy is someone else. As I said, I am here completely by accident."

"What? Not the son of Francisco Molinhem? Then who are you? Speak boy. Otherwise, we can't employ you and you must be on your way."

Filipe notices the girl from earlier. She's been standing there all the time, listening to the exchange. She interjects, "If I may Chef, was the Molinhem boy not expected some weeks ago? Perhaps he has no interest in the opportunity to work with one of the greatest chefs in Paris. If he has not presented himself already, then why do we expect him to do so in the future?"

Chef Francesc is amused by her transparent attempt at manipulating him and humours her, "Perhaps you have a good point Tereza. And perhaps you are misguided, hmm? I suppose I shall have permission from you to hire him?"

Filipe and the girl glance at each other, before Filipe says, "My father will not have to give permission. He was killed not three days ago by bandits here in Paris."

"I'm sorry to hear that. Then find your mother. Bring her here so she can speak for you."

"I cannot sir…Chef. She is also dead."

"Well, this is disgraceful. Who is looking after you then? Who can give their permission for your education to continue under my instruction? There is the matter of the law, you understand."

Filipe lowers his eye and thinks for a moment, before answering as sincerely as he can, "I don't believe there is anyone."

"Well, this is a tough situation. How shall we resolve this. You are already in debt to me for the destruction you have wrought. Here is what we shall do. You shall stay and work for me. I shall pay you in food and shelter. You shall sleep in the back, next to Tereza's room. She is a good neighbour, and a fortunate interlocutor who has already once come to your rescue. Perhaps one day you will have a chance to repay the kindness."

Then he turns his haughty gaze on the girl, "He's your responsibility now. I expect you to have him ready by tomorrow morning. We start early."

With that he marches out, turning his head slightly to address Filipe one last time, "Work hard and you have the opportunity to change your life. Now help Tereza to clean up this mess." Filipe feels light-headed. Is this a dream? For the first time in days he feels like he has a purpose.

"Yes Chef!"

Heart and soul are the most important ingredients to any dish.

CHAPTER 14

Turkish delight

"What's sauce for the goose may be sauce for the
gander, but it is not necessarily sauce for the chicken,
the duck, the turkey, or the Guinea hen."
Old proverb

As Paris poached in a swirl of its own political juices, a mini revolution was taking place inside the kitchen of Chef Francesc Alain Petit. Here Filipe was discovering Francesc's world of cuisine and all that went with it. The chef was the undisputed god in his little universe. Nothing happened here without the express knowledge or permission of the all-seeing creator, the veritable life-force of the kitchen. As Filipe gradually came to learn, the art of great cuisine was about more than merely putting ingredients into a pot, or an oven, and waiting for something to happen. Indeed, cooking was as much about feeding the stomach as it was all the other senses; the eye, the nose, even the ear should be surprised and delighted by the exotic dance that played itself out on the stage of Francesc's theatre.

Filipe had never imagined food as a fine commodity to be enjoyed in the way people enjoy fine clothes. But just as his grandfather's Dhakar Muslin was transformed into a garment fit for the queen herself, here the finest ingredients were transformed into food fit for a king.

Francesc's kingdom consists of several spheres of operation, little fiefdoms, if you will, each under their own banner – restaurant, pâtisserie, confectionery. These are words Filipe has never heard before, but as Tereza explains it to him, a restaurant is just like a tavern, but without the endless drinking and drunkenness; a pâtisserie is like a bakery, and the confectionary is dedicated to making only sweet food. Even more remarkably for the young ingenu, he discovers that people can come there even when they are not hungry and take food away with them for consumption whenever they wanted it.

It was no wonder the great chef's devoted customers and followers referred to him as a chef among the chefs, food sommelier, a confectioner du monde. Here was an artist at the height of his experimental and creative powers. And a man with no small vision for the future of his art.

"Felipe, this is the vanguard of cooking," he proclaims in a swirl of his own steam, "what we do here represents the very spirit of modern French cuisine. Future generations will emulate our methods and Paris will be known as the cradle of gastronomy, not just in France, but of the world."

The very notion of it sounds crazy to young Filipe; but to watch Francesc hard at work was to believe anything was possible. And work they did. Day in and day out. Hard work was as important as any other ingredient, and in this regard, success was assured.

Little by little Filipe grows in competence and confidence. His progress does not go unnoticed. Tereza, originally sceptical of the talents of the destroyer-of-tarts, has to acknowledge his aptitude and willingness to learn. Even the Great Grumpy Chef himself seems pleased with his protégé's progress. "Heita!" exclaims Tereza. "I think Chef Petit has found his petit chef." It's clear that she has taken a liking to the boy. Despite her own misgivings about his obvious lowly origins, she detects a curious intellect in him. He's the friend and brother she never had. And he returns the affection, treating her gently and with respect.

Francesc, noting the boy's gentle nature, opines, "you know Tereza, many people of above average aptitudes show themselves this way. A gentle soul has nothing to prove. There is no hatred or animosity towards those less fortunate. Filipe has these qualities. I believe his suffering has caused him to mature faster than the other little brats from wealthy families, who even when they become adults, still behave like spoiled children."

The chef, despite his seemingly limitless energy in the kitchen, is getting older, and he knows it. He has not found the time to produce an heir. Perhaps this boy, who has come into his life by a lucky accident will be the one to carry on his legacy. Tereza jokes that they are already like father and son, two peas in a pod. Indeed, Francesc does feel like this is the son he never had. And Filipe, for his part, is happy to think of the old man as a second father.

The budding chef is like a sponge, absorbing everything he can from the Old Master, as he and Tereza cheekily call him in reference to the masters of the guilds of painters and artists.

*

* *

It becomes a fixture of their activities that they set out together each morning in search of ingredients for the day's dishes. Their first stop is invariably an ancient oriental emporium, run by a long-time friend of Francesc's, a man whom the chef refers to only as Dear Dhortu. Dhortu is a coffee-coloured man of uncertain provenance, "Half Indian, half French and half Arab," as Francesc liked to say. Here they start the day with cups of dark Turkish coffee out of a pot the man called a Cezve, and soft sugary confections flavoured with rosewater, or bergamot, which, Dhortu referred to as his secret Delights.

The shop is a feast of visual and olfactory input. Multi-coloured spices are heaped in jute bags alongside baskets of fresh vegetables. Strings of garlic and chillies hang drying above them. There are also various kinds of meat and fish curing in coarse sea salt and crushed peppercorns. On the counter are rainbows of innumerable powders. The effect is like being inside an extravagant oil painting, whose excited artist has made their brushstrokes to amuse and delight not only the eyes, but also the nose.

These morning sessions serve as inspiration and set the tone for the rest of the pre-lunch expeditions. Invigorated by the Turkish coffee, the pair would visit the markets, testing

134

and tasting the wares of the various vendors and planning their recipes.

Filipe learns that garlic comes in several different shapes, colours and sizes, and that its cousin, the French onion, is in fact part of an entire extended family whose ranks include scallions, leeks, and chives. There are things that grow under the ground and above it. Things that reach skyward and things that spread out along the ground. Each has its own special properties and place in the kitchen. The array of ingredients to be found here is as overwhelming as it is exciting.

As much as Chef Francesc finds inspiration in the markets of Paris, he is also a great believer in looking beyond France for inspiration. His collection of cookbooks from as far away as China and the Malay Archipelago is as precious to him as the gardens at Versailles. Foreign food cultures were not to be avoided, rather they were to be explored and embraced at every opportunity. "There are great food discoveries to be made, Filipe, if we open our eyes and our hearts to the opportunity. The world is a big adventure for those who seek knowledge, but very small for those who already think they know everything."

"For millennia man ate what was around him. What the climate allowed in one place was different in another. But then people began to move from one place to another, bringing their knowledge of different food with them. What would the world be like without new tastes to discover? It is important as chefs, for us to seek out new places and bring back food knowledge with us.

"Imagine the idea of an indigenous tribe called the Mayans, all the way in the New World, who created flat breads made from corn. In Asia they have as many ways to prepare rice as there are rice grains in a barrel. Some cultures take as their staple beans. In Africa they favour gourds and roots such as manioc and casava. Here in Europe, we have wheat and potatoes.

"Eggs are a staple in all cultures, but the best chickens are undoubtedly French; I tell you, there is nothing in the whole of the world quite like our very own poulet de Bresse.

"Even the red meat from cows is different from place to place, depending on how they are raised and what they eat; some have more fat, while others are naturally more tender. In some parts of the world, they salt and dry the meat to preserve it for eating during the winter months. The cuisine of the Gypsies is rich in game and is made using creative preparations from the intersection of Europe and Asia. In the east and the north, they prepare and eat fish raw, or preserved in vinegar. We know that certain religions forbid the eating of underwater creatures and swine. There are even places in the world where the men hunt crocodiles and snakes for food, as well as other animals that we would not even think of as being edible."

The chef's face is animated with enthusiasm as he talks about the thing that has consumed him with passion for more years than he can remember. He wants to pass all his wonderment onto this young version of himself. Becoming self-aware, he pauses and takes a breath.

"All this is to say, Filipe, French cuisine may be the best in the world, but the French way is only one in a universe full of diversity. We must not limit ourselves to such a parochial attitude that we are unreasoning of other ways of doing and being. We must learn to understand the ways of other cultures.

"There are many French who despise anything that is not of France, looking down on even our neighbours, the Italians, and the Spanish."

Filipe notices that the tone of this conversation has grown more serious. "We're not talking about food anymore, are we?"

"No. Indeed we are not. You are an astute young man. Today we shall visit a new butcher. A man perhaps not as forward looking as we are. Let me do the talking. We must avoid them hearing your Piedmontese accent today, hmm? There is a growing undercurrent of nationalism, and politics sours the taste of good food."

That is the first and last time the subject of Filipe's heritage is spoken between the two of them, save for the occasional correction to Filipe's French pronunciation.

Filipe's studies on the influence of food on the human body.

CHAPTER 15

A happy place

"Nobody has ever killed anybody else
while eating a mouthful of cake."
Filipe Borriana Francisconi

The weeks go by in a blur for the young kitchen apprentice. The bond that's forming between Francesc, Filipe, and Tereza is more that of a family than chef and kitchen staff. Despite the long hours of effort, and the exacting standards of the chef, or perhaps precisely because of those high standards, Filipe and Tereza are becoming a great team in the kitchen. They are a squad. They are friends. They have each other's backs.

One night, on her way to get a cup of water, Tereza hears a strange sound coming from Filipe's room. Soon she's knocking on Francesc's bedroom door, waking him from a dream in which angels are inserting garlic and rosemary into flying roast lambs. He grumpily opens the door to find the girl, candle in hand wearing a nightgown and a worried expression. She speaks quietly and quickly, noting the chef's cranky countenance. "It's Filipe. I found him crying in his room. This is not the first time – I think there is something wrong. We need to find out what it is."

Still half asleep, the chef splashes water on his face from a small basin and grabs the oil lamp to illuminate the corridors of the old shophouse. Reaching the boy's room, they knock and quietly call out, "Filipe." After what seems like an eternity, but in reality is barely a minute, the door cracks open and Filipe's face peeps out. The chef enters and sits on the side of the bed then motions to Filipe to perch himself on the nearby stool. The room is neat, with everything arranged just so – *mise en place* – appropriate for a budding chef, thinks Francesc.

He puts his hand out and lifts the boy's chin to get a better look. Filipe's eyes are red from crying. He's clearly embarrassed.

"Filipe, there's no shame in a man crying, let alone a boy of such sensitive temperament such as you are. What ails you? Out with it. What is causing you such anguish?"

Filipe takes a deep breath, perhaps to summon the courage to talk. "I miss my father. And my mother, who left me when I was very young. She was always my hero, Francesc, since I can remember. We always got along so well. After she died, I was lucky enough to find my father. But he was taken away, too. Everyone important gets taken away … my grandfather…" the sobs rob him of his breath and of his voice. Maybe death stalks me because I have broken God's laws. But to survive, I had to kill. That's why God is punishing me."

Through tears and hot snot, he relates the misadventure at Francois Pierre's ranch when he and his father killed the bandits, and the skirmish at the city gate on the outskirts of Paris.

The astonished Francesc does his best to stay coherent in the face of such revelations, pointing out that far from being cursed, Filipe's actions demonstrate that God is protecting him, else he should be dead himself. The bandits got what they deserved. The very fact that he, Filipe, is still alive, is nothing short of a blessing and a miracle.

The boy is not so easily consoled and mumbles something about predestination and divine retribution and living in the shadow of God's wrath. How many nights has he cried himself to sleep, longing for his grandfather, for his mother and father, the weight of loneliness suffocating him inside? Through sobs he vows never to kill another living being again.

How can a boy so young be burdened with such demons? Francesc, overwhelmed with emotion at the distress of his young ward, puts his arm around Filipe and says, "You cannot…must not…blame yourself for the past. Those dangerous tales are behind us, they are not part of your life now.

"I see not the urchin who upset the tart cart. I see a young man eager to learn. A young man with an enormous talent and an extraordinary future. More importantly, I have found a friend. A son, even. Although I do not dare have the audacity to suggest that I can replace your real parents. But what I can say for sure is that you have found a home. And you are safe here."

The words are of great comfort to a boy who in recent times had experienced such uncertainty. It is true that he, Filipe, has come to think of the old man as more than just the boss of the kitchen. The chef looks deeply into the boy's eyes and hugs him with a tenderness that only mothers and fathers have for their children.

*

* *

It's said that great ideas strike when we least expect them to. For Filipe, the moment comes one morning as he's creaming butter and sugar for incorporation into a pâte sablée that will later form the basis for a rainbow-coloured series of fruit tarts.

Nobody has ever killed anybody else while eating a mouthful of cake.

It's a crazy thought. But no crazier than anything else he's been through, so why not? Breathlessly he reveals his BIG IDEA to Chef Francesc. "What if we could use the power of cooking to end the world's wars? Have we not seen how happy food makes people? All quarrels, disputes and disagreements melt away the face of the joy that a good meal brings. Happy men don't fight and kill each other; full stomachs do not leap at each other's throats. They resolve their problems wisely, with conversation and reason."

Francesc puts down the paring knife he has been using to fillet a large catfish most recently from the Seine, "What?"

"Remember the Indian book you once showed me? The one we used for inspiration for exotic and well-seasoned dishes?"

"Yes. I think so. But…?"

"Well, you said that Indian people used food as a way to treat their ills and achieve inner peace. Nirvana, you said it was called."

"Food, yes, and meditation."

"Yes! Exactly. And do you remember the illustration of the yogi with his hand on his stomach? The book said that was where good energy came from."

Francesc grins, happy that the boy is finding a deeper purpose among the pots, pans, and paraphernalia of the kitchen. "Yes, I think I understand where you are going with this. If you want harmony between people, you must start with their stomachs. A full stomach means a happy heart. This is the dream of every chef. To make people happy. But I never thought of it in the way you have just articulated it."

World peace as a direct result of cooking? he thinks. Cuisine conquering the hearts of the conquerors. What an audacious thought. And why not? A grand ideal of harmony born out of the naïve thinking of a boy whose life had almost been taken from him. Francesc cannot help but love Filipe all the more. "What a crazy thought. Well, I believe I am just crazy enough. Yes, I will make you the best chef in the world. And through cooking you and I will conquer the hearts and imagination of everyone who is fortunate enough to taste it."

The boy smiles through tears of joy. It's a smile of peace and eternal gratitude. It's also the smile of a boy becoming a man with a purpose.

Two are now joined in one goal — to make peace through the stomachs of men.

Napoleon's Grande Armée stamped its mark onto the European consciousness.

CHAPTER 16

Aliche

"I know I'm an acquired taste - I'm anchovies.
And not everybody wants those hairy little things."
Tori Amos

The early days of the First French Republic are a heady casserole of enlightened ideas and competing political spiciness. Aristocratic society has all but been destroyed, and the feudal structure, with the privileges that had created such inequity, is crumbling like a weeks-old shortcrust. The unbalanced political power of the church has been demolished. New social perspectives and structures begin to emerge. A new social contract speaks of liberté, égalité, fraternité.

But the enlightened ideas of a post-revolutionary society have not yet coalesced into the happy peace they promised. France finds itself at war both with its neighbours and internally with itself. Many citizens are wary of venturing out, lest they get caught up in one of the many exotic radical movements of the time.

The restaurant has managed to hold onto its most loyal clientele, but the steady stream of hungry diners who had kept Francesc, Filipe and Tereza on their feet has trickled off. Despite this, the trio are as busy as ever. What has increased, interestingly, is the number of requests for food to be brought to various private homes and taverns around the area. Their cooking is still in demand; only the logistics of getting it into the bellies of the people who want it has changed.

"I'm going to call it Restaurant Deliveries," Francesc announces one morning. I predict that this will become the fashion for restaurants like ours in the future. Filipe's young mind is off at a canter. "Well, I understand deliveries…because I used to do deliveries with my father. But I always wanted to ask you why you call it a restaurant. When I first came here, I had never heard the name before. But now it seems like it's one more important thing to understand."

Francesc smiles, "Ah, Filipe, ever the curious one. I will tell you. The story is simple – I borrowed the name from a friend who ran an establishment, not unlike this one, next to a military weapons factory. The factory work was hard – smelting metal, making heavy equipment – and the men were tired after the day's work. My friend's establishment created a special broth that was said to restore the strength of the factory workers. If you think carefully about it, it seems logical that the place where you went to eat a restorative broth would be called a restaurant. Well, the word caught on, and now a restaurant is a place that restores the health and well-being of the people who come there.

"As I said, Filipe, cooking is about invention. And today we have not only one invention, but two – the restaurant AND

146

deliveries. Perhaps we will be like Julius Caesar supplying his generals across the whole of the Roman Empire."

*

* *

Their culinary journey takes them across the world and into realms past and present, real and imaginary. Together they explore one kingdom's predilection for pork cuts, and how this would never do for the French. How the Romans had no culinary prejudices, and perhaps became the greatest civilisation the world had ever seen because of it. How Christians eschewed red meat on a Friday. How the Jews avoided shellfish. How certain foods were bound to a region, like sausages from Calabria, cheeses from Roquefort and Tarta de Santiago from Galicia.

From that point forward the two of them divide their time between the day-to-day operations of the various detachments of Restaurant Petit, and the ongoing program of culinary experimentation that is de rigueur in the finest kitchens. They pore over, and take inspiration from, the many books that are as integral a part of the kitchen as the myriad copper pots and wooden spoons, and they scour the markets for new ingredients to invent exotic new dishes and recipes based on what they have read. "Reading gives us ideas," says Francesc, "but cooking is the real test of our skill."

Not all their experiments are successful, but their voyage of discovery has been joined in earnest. And one thing is becoming clear – Filipe is developing a complex and intricate palate, his combinations of ingredients and cooking methods sometimes surprising even Francesc with their sophistication.

*

* *

One morning Francesc greets Filipe and Tereza in the kitchen and enthusiastically announces that they are going to experiment with making a new kind of flattened bread, the recipe for which comes via an old acquaintance who lived under the shadow of a once fiery Vesuvius, a mountain that was so hungry it devoured an entire city.

The recipe calls for the bread to be seasoned with anchovies, little oily fish with a big flavour. Francesc gives Filipe a masterclass on the preparation of the slender little blue *aliche*, packing them into brining jars for the up-to-year-long process of curing them using only salt, oil and water, that results in the characteristic savoury flavour.

Soon the conversation wanders onto other ways of preserving food using vinegar instead of water, and a multitude of spices complementary to salt. Filipe is already familiar with the bright peppery kick of peppercorns, the zesty zing of mustard seeds and the fiery oomph of dried chilli. And of course, the bay leaves that are fundamental to the bouquet garni that is the staple of any self-respecting chef.

As their bread dough rises in a warm corner of the kitchen, they get to know other spices; Allspice from the Caribbean, with its hint of warmth; cloves with their sweet bitterness; coriander with its aromatic citrusy quality; and ginger, one of the cornerstone aromatics in Asian cooking. All have their own special place in the cuisines of the world.

After a time, the bread has risen to Francesc's satisfaction, forming itself a somewhat sticky little ball. To Filipe's amusement, rather than placing it in a loaf pan, as is customary, the older chef presses the dough with his hands, to form a roughly circular flat cake.

"What do you call this?" asks Filipe.

"Well, since we are exploring the world through cooking, perhaps we shall call it pan de *pisado*, the stepped-on-bread after the Spanish word *pisar*, which means to step on."

They place a liberal amount of previously cured anchovies on the flat dough, along with finely chopped garlic, rosemary, and salt.

"The anchovies will give it a savoury flavour that I wager will be delicious," says Francesc. He winks at Filipe, who has a somewhat sceptical look on his face, "Tereza will be our taste-tester."

They bake their invention at a high heat until the edges puff up and become crispy and a little charred. Once it's out of the oven they drizzle a little Moroccan olive oil on the bread and cut it into pieces.

Filipe is hesitant at first, being somewhat wary of the unbridled vigour of the anchovies, but after seeing Tereza's delight at the newly created bread, he joins in and finds himself quickly and happily going for a second slice before the others gobble what's left of the dish.

They all declare the experiment a roaring success. So, too, do the customers. The new *pisar* very quickly becomes a legend in its own lunchtime.

They also try out sweet pastries made from potato dough and cream whipped together with sugar, with Filipe learning that the sweet recipes can be as demanding as the savoury dishes.

Little by little they expand their confidence and their repertoire, gaining a reputation for fine cooking among private houses and taverns alike. Such is their popularity, that most mornings the pair are compelled to set out early to visit various butchers and merchants in other parts of Paris if they are to meet the demand for the orders of the day.

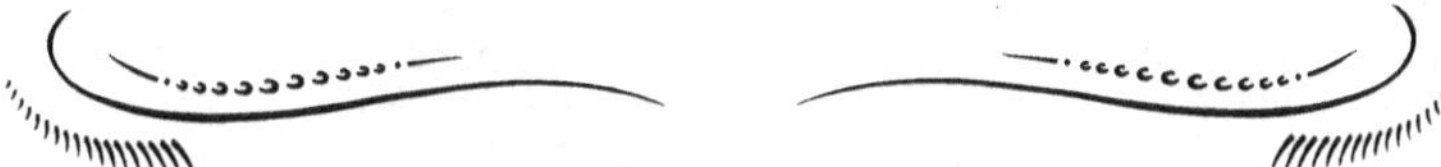

Preparations for the grand banquet.

CHAPTER 17

An invitation

"And I like large parties. They're so intimate.
At small parties there isn't any privacy."
Jordan Baker from The Great Gatsby

The routine at Restaurant Petit is interrupted one late autumn day with the arrival of a courier carrying an ornately decorated letter addressed to the Chefs of Chez Francesc. The despatch turns out to be an invitation to cook for a banquet and dance to be held at the famous Chateau Blosseau, home of doyenne of the social scene and inimitable hostess, Madame la Boar, in honour of a newly promoted young French general.

Along with the invitation is a service contract, which Francesc signs and hands back to the courier. And although he doesn't like to leave his establishment unattended, he understands the necessity to maintain his place in society. Let's face it, esteem and reputation aside, these parties are good for the coffers and pay for a lot of experimentation back in the engine room of the good ship Chez Petit.

Parties and banquets are not uncommon. It might even be observed that these events have taken on a highly competitive flavour among the houses and chateaux of Paris and its surrounds, as they vie to outdo each other with ever-more lavish banquets and dances. Francesc's reputation among those who can afford such affairs makes him a highly sought-after commodity, and the chefs and cooks who staff the kitchens of the great mansions, as well as the ladies who preside over them, are in awe of Francesc for his ability to produce legendary feasts that have mouths salivating and tongues wagging for weeks after the food has been devoured, the drinks drunk, and everyone returned safely to their homes.

Francesc's first course of action is to call a meeting of his trusty kitchen lieutenants, Filipe and Tereza. "It's silly season again," he announces. "Blosseau is hosting a party and the invitation you saw me receive came directly from Madame la Boar herself. We'll need to pull out all the stops on this one. All the usual suspects will be there, of course, but I believe there'll also some very illustrious guests, and possibly even some notable dignitaries from France's allies in Europe.

"Of course, there is no question that we are the best cuisiniers in all of Paris. We must show them that they have made the correct choice in trusting us with this work." He claps his hands together in a cloud of flour, "this will be our glorious moment, the moment we conquer palates and win allies through food. There's no time to waste. Planning starts now."

Tereza and Filipe give each other a subtle nod. Francesc's enthusiasm is infectious, but it can become a runaway train if not steered correctly. They sit at the long wooden worktable and brainstorm what and how they intend to cook, what they will need to prepare in advance, what must be cooked in their own kitchen and transported to the mansion, and what can be cooked and assembled in the Blosseau kitchen. And for how long.

There's also the matter of provisioning to be considered. Some ingredients will have to be obtained and hung days in advance. Some will need to be put on ice. Others will need to be procured fresh, a day before the banquet, or even the day of. Orders will have to go out to trusted merchants in advance to make sure that there are no surprises.

Finally, there's the logistics of the operation to consider. The how, where, when and by whom, the feast in its various stages of deconstruction will travel from Chez Petit to Chateau Blosseau.

It's all hands on deck.

*

* *

The first order of preparation involves the charcuterie. They begin the process of curing, salting, smoking, grinding, pureeing, brining, and sieving for an ambitious menu of pork, fish, poultry, game birds and veal.

Six medium sized pigs and two wild boars are slowly roasted in the course of twenty-four hours and allowed to cool in the cellar. The meat is then placed into several large terrines and lard poured over it to preserve it and keep in the delicate flavour.

A hunter has provided them with four deer, already cleaned. They cut off the excess fat and coat the meat with salt to tenderise it. This, too, they let cool in the cellar before moving to the next part of the preparation.

While Francesc fusses with the giant smoking oven – a temperamental beast if ever there was one – Filipe and Tereza coat the venison liberally with olive oil, then lavish it with a crust of secret herbs and spices and wrap it in muslin for the final touch before it disappears into the smoker for days.

Using his seemingly endless network of suppliers, Francesc has manged to get his hand on two boxes of salted cod from Norway. These they put though the somewhat counter-intuitive process of de-salting, which uses rock salt to extract the salt from the fish itself. It involves covering the cod in coarse salt and soaking them for two days in fresh water, completely replacing the water every five to six hours.

There will also be a mountain of nuts, olives, dates, Turkish Delights and other confectionaries from their old friend Dhortu.

Francesc calculates that they will need to bring four carts full of prepared food to the banquet as well as an additional two carts with uncooked supplies for cooking at the château.

Vegetables and fruit will be delivered directly to Blosseau on the day of the great feast.

Chateau Blosseau.

CHAPTER 18

Layer cake

"Baroque is the most theatrical of styles,
for it is the least logical and the most ornamental."
Mario Praz

The date of the big event is set for late October in the year of our lord 1795. Francesc and Filipe arrive at Chateau Blosseau a day before the banquet proper to supervise proceedings, and importantly, to see that the more complex preparations are begun in time to be ready for the feast.

While no Versailles, Chateau Blosseau is nevertheless a striking building. It's a veritable layer-cake of Gallo Roman strength and French Baroque extravagance. Strong, solid foundations laid by Julius Caesar's armies. Walls and ground-level in the Frankish style with solid beams and heavy, fitted stone propping up the Baroque style second and third storey *corps de logis* that were added a thousand years later. All crowned with a high, sloping mansard roof.

The mixture of styles is testament to millennia of social and cultural development reaching as far back as the Celts. As each civilisation was replaced by its successor, the new masters of the land destroyed what they didn't need, built upon what was useful, and kept what they could, while altering or reconstructing what they needed.

The current incarnation of the mansion is a typical specimen in an area that came to be populated by wealthy French Nobles who hired renowned architects and builders to transform these forts into mansions. Such was the scale of their vision that even great rivers were diverted to create lush gardens and magnificent ornamental playgrounds for the idle rich.

*

**

Yawning sentinels grumpily open the gate to the early arrival of the forward party consisting of the chefs and their small train of wagons. Francesc and Filipe are suitably taken with the grandeur of the place and hardly notice the guards' protestations at being too early and too noisy.

Passing through the main entrance they look at each other and continue in awe for a minute or two. Filipe thinks back to the last time he visited such a beautiful place. He recalls accompanying his grandfather to a cathedral in Milan. The old man had gone there at the invitation of two old friends of his, Giuseppe Perego and Giuseppe Bini, respected builders who had needed a craftsman skilled in marble production.

The cathedral had been in a never-ending state of construction since the 1300s and even had its own "marble factory", in the form of Candoglia quarry. The ongoing building and renovations required the maintenance of the marble-cutting and polishing equipment on-site. Filipe had spent three formative months watching his grandfather work on one of the most incredible projects in all of Christendom.

Francesc says what's on both of their minds, "We'll need to be at our best if we're going to prove ourselves worthy of such a place."

They travel through the curlicued and manicured gardens for a hundred meters or so, past the highly stylised and symmetrical shapes of the flowerbeds. In the weak morning sun, the autumn colours of the trees along the driveway make the sky look like it's on fire, while vying for their attention with what green remains of the box-cut hedges that make up the characteristic "embroidered" patterns that are typical of the Baroque gardens of the time.

Even Chef Francesc, who is used to the pomp and trappings of French society, is impressed. He refocuses his thoughts on the carts laden with provisions and the task ahead. He goes over the important details in his head. The steady figure of Filipe sitting next to him is a reassuring presence.

Ahead, the tree-lined driveway bifurcates with one path forking off to the front of the mansion, where guests will be received in the not-too-distant future, and the other leading to the back of the mansion, where the kitchen and service functions are located. In his pre-occupied state, Francesc takes a wrong turn and finds himself leading the little train of wagons toward the main reception.

A not insignificant amount of confusion ensues as a guard tries to head them off. "Halt, I say." He continues in a mocking tone, "Just where do you think you are headed?

This way is for ladies and gentlemen. Servants and delivery boys are to go around to the back."

Francesc is none too happy with being lumped in with the so-called help. And in any case, it's too late to turn back. He draws himself up in that very French way of his and is about to speak, when Madame la Boar clucks into view.

"You there. Guard! Yes you. This is no ordinary delivery wagon. This is Chef Francesc Alain Petit, the greatest chef in Paris, and a dear friend of the household. Kindly refrain from taking that tone with him. There is no cause for war among ourselves; there will be enough of that once the generals arrive, yes?"

"My dear Francesc," she greets him like a long-lost cousin and glares at the soldier, "well, this is not very elegant. It seems some of us do not know our manners. Let them pass without further ado."

The soldier, perhaps out of stubbornness, or perhaps simply not wanting to break any rules, stiffens.

Mme la Boar affixes him with a haughty look, "Pay attention man. Some rules are meant to be broken. And I am the lady of the house after all. So, I may invent or break any of the rules I desire. Do you understand?"

Some of the military bearing goes out of the man as he seems to deflate somewhat. He lowers his guard and waves them on.

They enter through the main doors into a vast reception area. A black and white chequered floor like a giant chess board stretches off towards a magnificent central staircase that rises to a mezzanine, where two black and gold marble urns stand guard like giant chess pieces, as the staircase splits off to either side and climbs to the first-floor salon. A huge fireplace dominates the centre of the mezzanine, flanked by red silk chairs. Above it hangs an enormous painting of a great battle between Arab warriors, set against a vast desert landscape. Elsewhere the walls are festooned with oil paintings depicting all manner of dramatic subject matter.

Below and to the back of the staircase, behind discreet entrances, are the guards' quarters, service-areas and of course, the kitchens, where the chef's party should have ended up if they had been paying attention. Never mind, they're here now, and the unshakable Mme la Boar simply pulls them along like a human caravan towards the kitchen area where an expectant staff awaits their introduction.

"Girls and boys," she chants happily, "allow me to introduce to you the great Chef Francesc Alain Petit and his assistant…" Francesc gives her a look that says, this is more than a mere assistant, and she quickly corrects course, "should I say co-conspirator in the kitchen," giving Filipe a cheeky wink.

"Mesdames et Messieurs," Francesc, determined to avoid any misunderstanding at this early stage, adopts a formal tone "let me be clear, Filipe is one of the finest chefs in all of Paris. Do not be fooled by his young age. You would be well advised to heed his instructions. Perhaps you might even learn a thing or two."

Filipe, already blushing at the chef's words, notices that one of the young maids has been making eyes at him from the back of the congregated staff and feels himself redden to a crimson embarrassment.

Luckily everyone is preoccupied with the importance of the moment and his awkwardness goes unnoticed.

The Madame, not to be outdone, retakes the floor with a clap of her pink, jewel-encrusted hands, "Bom, bom. Great things are expected of us all. History is about to be made – follow the chefs' instructions and we shall not disappoint." With that, she exits with a flourish, leaving behind the faint odour of sandalwood and citrus.

The kitchen staff shuffle nervously in the presence of their temporary commander-in-chief, adjusting clothing and pulling at their aprons with quick hand movements. Francesc puts them at ease with a quick smile and entreats them to relax. "Right, let's get the provisions from the wagons and see where we are, shall we. No need to rush – slow and steady wins the race. We have all morning to plan our course of attack, and if we do our work properly, success will follow."

Outside the kitchen, in the yard that opens to the back of the estate, a certain lieutenant, Gilles Trusseau, has been watching the proceedings with a mixture of curiosity and suspicion. How is it that this bunch had arrived through the front of the house, and not the service entrance, as was customary? He calls the guard who had been talking to Madame la Boar earlier over to interrogate him. "Who are those uncouth figures who have the audacity to go against everything that is civilised?"

His colleague looks around nervously for any sign of the lady of the house might be within earshot and shrugs. This is not a conversation he wants to have with the lieutenant, a man not known for his patience. "Chefs, as I understand it. Friends of the Madame. Here for the big party."

"Keep an eye on them. There are still too many loyal to those foul Bourbons. I want to know where they go, who they speak to and what they do. Even after they leave here. Especially after they leave here."

The two men pretended to be examining some piece of equipment, while trying to overhear any useful snippets of information.

The two chefs pretended to write menus on a blackboard in the kitchen while trying to overhear what the guards are talking about.

It's the perfect start to a banquet that promises politics, intrigue and of course, good food.

Francesc and Filipe admire their expressive works.

CHAPTER 19

Mise en place

"Strange to see how a good dinner and
feasting reconciles everybody."
Samuel Pepys

Chef Petit assembles his kitchen brigade to run through the stations; dishwashers I want everything scrubbed like your lives depend on it. I saw a few pans that looked like they were growing their own herbs.

Porters, make sure you learn your routes, I don't want any collisions or accidents. And make sure storage is kept clear of any obstacles.

Prep cooks, over here with me, I need your full attention as we go over the menu.

Mise-en-place kicks off with Francesc demonstrating the different knife skills required for the dishes he has planned. Carrots Julienne. Onions *fine brunoise*. Endive and delicate greens, chiffonade. He explains how he wants the salads washed and presented. How to properly peel the garlic, and how to clean the leeks to ensure no sand remains within the folds of the leaves.

Felipe, meanwhile, does a thorough reconnoitre of the kitchen. At the heart of the operation, he finds three wood-burning ovens and five cookers. The ovens are a curiosity that seems in keeping with the eclectic composition of the chateau itself, in that they are Roman cob-ovens – made from clay, sugar-paste, corn husk fibre and hay. The romans knew how to incorporate compressed corn husks into the clay bricks as a reinforcing agent, giving them increased strength. The sugar was added because it vitrified with heat, creating superior insulation and a structure that was incredibly efficient at radiating heat within its cooking belly. These ovens are oldies, but definitely goodies.

The working area consists of two long, sturdy tables and a large, solid butcher's block made from Hungarian Oak, standing on robust carved legs. The top is well worn after a life of service under the meat cleaver that even now stands ready for action, its sharpened edge biting into a corner of the hard wood.

The kitchen is elsewhere similarly well-accoutred. There are any number of saucepans of all shapes, sizes and descriptions hanging in strategic positions above the various workstations. Tucked away under the counters Filipe finds cauldrons for boiling soups and broths large enough to feed an army. On shelves and in drawers is a veritable arsenal of ladles, wooden spoons, whisks, knives, cleavers, spatulas, tenderising hammers, meat-grinders, pliers and even a few tools that look like they rather belonged in the Conciergerie. One curiosity he's never seen before is a flint fire-lighter. It consists of a small magnesium rod that produces sparks when struck with the back of a kitchen knife. "An invention of the Ottomans in Constantinople, so I believe," says one of the kitchen maids, showing Filipe the ornately carved and inlaid handle, as she demonstrates its use.

Filipe is in his element. This is a kitchen that he can make sing.

Francesc calls everyone over for a final briefing. "Ladies and gentlemen, your moment to shine has come. We will make this a banquet at Blosseau that no one will forget. We will be serving four main dishes, which are to be placed on the main tables in the dining hall. Alongside these, for the young couples who wish to dance and socialise, we will be serving an assortment of lighter dishes – appetisers, crudites and other *amuse-gueules*. You all remember your stations, I hope. Any questions to me or Filipe. Now who's in charge of the cakes, sweets and tea?"

Everyone smiles and claps their hands. The maids scurry about excitedly.

*

* *

Outside, carriages have been arriving in a steady stream. The sound of happy voices and laughter is added to the already charged atmosphere. From above them in one of the salons, the sound of a chamber orchestra warming up joins the already pleasant hubbub of crackling fires, bubbling water, clanking of pots and footsteps and voices echoing to and fro.

While all this is happening the two chefs begin to place the starters onto the great trays that will convey them up to the guests. Delicate Asian style dumplings filled with shredded meat and cabbage in a light ginger and sesame paste. An array of hams, salamis, smoked meats, and sausages that had been prepared back at Chez Petit. Cheeses and candied fruits, nuts and dates.

There is an entire section devoted to poultry – smoked, roasted, preserved in aspic and otherwise spectacularly presented. By far the centre of attraction is the dish called Suvorov's Pheasant, named after the great Russian general, hunter and eater (in no particular order), Aleksander Suvorov, whom Francesc had had the pleasure of meeting some years earlier. The recipe for Suvorov's Pheasant is simple enough, but the ingredients are far too rare and expensive for any mistakes to be made in its preparation. It calls for one large pheasant, hung by the neck for four days in summer, or a dozen in winter, to promote decomposition and fermentation so as to deepen and bring out the flavour, skinned and boned, seasoned only with salt, truffles and butter, and stuffed with foie gras.

Also on the menu is a not-so-simple bouillon de poulet, made with whole chicken carcasses, fresh ginger, Parisian mushrooms, sesame oil, white wine, leeks and onions.

*

* *

The noise from above signals that the party is in full swing. Filipe is surprised by a tug at his arm. Francesc pulls him aside with a wink and a smile and indicates that he should take off his apron and chef's hat. "Come and see how the guests are enjoying our handiwork." To Filipe's surprise and excitement Francesc gestures towards the stairs.

At the landing they pass through a pair of gilded doors into a large, long salon, and move to stand behind a set of ornately carved screens that have been carefully situated to conceal the comings and goings of the serving staff.

"Observe, Filipe."

The young man looks out onto a sea of beautiful, and beautifully dressed, people. Ladies and gentlemen in feathers and finery such as he has never witnessed. But what really transfixes him is the sight of all the food placed with an extravagant flourish on the long tables that have been arranged just so.

This is the fruit of so much hard work, not just today, but over the preceding weeks; and if he thought about it, the culmination of years practice and dedication.

His first grand banquet in his first great Chateau. Perhaps there were greater chefs in the world than them, but right now, Filipe feels like a king in a castle.

Everyone has outdone themselves in anticipation of the big event. Flower arrangements, feathers and plumes adorn every table. Mme La Boar's flamboyant eye for detail has turned the whole setting into something out of an oil painting; certainly, the food itself looks like it sprang from the imagination of the Dutch artist, Floris van Dijck, whose "Still Life of Grapes and Cheese" coincidently hangs in an anteroom somewhere near the kitchen.

Felipe's eyes grow wide at the sight of such splendiferous extravagance.

On a table on the far side of the room a colourful stuffed pheasant looks like it is about to gobble a tray of canapés. Beneath its feet the table is festooned with bread, cakes, caviar, quail eggs, candied citrus peels, jellies, sweets, puddings and a multitude of other delights.

Next to it, a table carries an assortment of French cheeses and the charcuterie, exuberantly displayed. Salamis, hams, cold sausages, and smoked meats keep company with pots of pickled onions seasoned with Moroccan olive oil, strips of fresh yellow paprika and some special peppers, sourced from Dorthu himself.

Francesc notices his young partner's awe and wonder at the scene playing out before him.

"Observe well my young friend, for what you are witnessing here is about more than just the food. In the hands of an artist like Mme La Boar the food is elevated to another level. There is an almost architectural precision to it. She understands that people eat first with their eyes.

"To whet the appetite of the imagination, first impressions are everything. We do not fall in love with the quantity of food, as the old-fashioned thinking goes; but rather, it is the arrangement and beauty that captivates the senses. Quality, my boy, not quantity. That's the secret.

"It's this way in the animal kingdom too. Do we not see how the flower attracts the bee with its beauty and scent. Or how the Venus Flytrap's deadly beauty attracts insects.

"Once the eyes have feasted then the other senses are awakened. The eyes draw us in, and only then do the other senses take over."

From their hidden viewpoint behind the screens, the two chefs watch the happy procession of guests enjoying themselves. Aside from the food there is much else to feast the eyes upon. Beautiful women and elegant men, and plenty of plumage and pomp.

Suddenly the natural order of the party is disrupted by the appearance of a group of French soldiers accompanied by a man in ornate military regalia. He has about him an air of command. He surveys the room haughtily, acknowledging the polite greetings around him, until he catches Mme La Boar's eye.

"Cher," she swoops in and catches him by the arm, saying in a voice loud enough for everyone to hear, "welcome to your party Monsieur Bonaparte, or should I say General Bonaparte?" Those nearest Mme La Boar clap in appreciation, while others who had not witnessed his entrance now gather around to join in the spectacle. Soon a circle has formed around the General, who is holding court in the manner of a man born to it.

The hostess peels herself away from the throng and heads for the screens on the pretext of wanting to rearrange something. She has detected the presence of the two kitchen spies. "Gentlemen," she clucks, "come and meet our distinguished guest. Perhaps we can break into his little political circle for a moment and bring some culture to those bores. Did you know he was being promoted to the rank of Major General? Such an honour. We are making history tonight, and you are certainly part of it."

The hubbub coming from the men encircling the General shifts in tone. It seems that one of the women, an enigmatic and exotic young lady, has courageously broken through the outer defences. "Mr. Bonaparte," she ventures, deliberately and cheekily not using his military rank, "the ladies are asking after you. Perhaps the men wouldn't mind if we borrowed you for a while. We crave the freedom to interact with a man of your stature. Tell us of your heroic adventures…how you have conquered the courts of Europe… and the hearts …" She giggles saucily at the last bit.

An amused Mme la Boar winks at the two chefs, "Well, well, it seems the party is going even better than expected. The widow Josephine has found a new interest. Now if you'll excuse me, I must check on my guests. Bien joué messieurs. You have my gratitude."

Happily, the two chefs retreat to the safety of their kitchen to put the final touches to the main dishes. There is a moment when Filipe catches the General's eye; here is no ordinary man, thinks the young chef to himself. Even among such company he stands out. A conqueror whose power has been won, not merely given. Tonight, Napoleon is the lead player in his own drama, and all others mere supporting actors.

Filipe is left with the uncanny feeling that they will meet again.

Behold the fearsome vampire fish.

CHAPTER 20

Vampire Fish

"Lamprey's a most immodest diet:
You'll neither wake nor sleep in quiet"
John Gay, To a Young Lady, With Some Lampreys

The starters have been a roaring success, as evidenced by the increasingly raucous sounds from above, as well as reports from their various spies. Now, back in the kitchen Team Francesc is getting down to the very serious business of preparing for act two – and the stars of the show – the main dishes.

First on the menu is a gratinated *Brandade de Morue* utilising the cod that had mysteriously arrived from Norway and that they had painstakingly prepared back in their home kitchen.

Francesc's recipe follows the traditional Provencal method, where the fish is gently simmered in milk and then added to a mixture of cream, olive oil, bay leaves, garlic and thyme. Mashed potato is folded into the mixture, after which the whole thing is placed into a baking pan, topped with herbs and grated cheese, and baked until golden brown.

They will serve the dish with freshly baked country bread of their own making.

Next is *Porc al la Francesc*. Whole pig, slow roasted in especially manufactured giant copper terrines. The animals had been marinaded in orange juice, champagne and rosemary prior to making their journey to Chateau Blosseau. The skins were liberally rubbed with salt, pepper, garlic, crushed mustard and secret spices from Dhortu's emporium. Kitchen assistants had spent the better part of seven hours basting the skin with a mixture of lard and other secret ingredients until the outer layers of fat had formed into perfectly caramelised crackling.

Porc al Francesc is followed by a unique speciality dreamed up especially for the occasion – *venaison à deux mains*, or venison by the hand of two chefs. The meat had been prepared back at the restaurant. First the deer were stuffed with a mixture of oats, tomatoes, whole king-oyster mushrooms, carrots, leeks, quail eggs, pitted green olives and lots of virgin olive oil from Morocco. Beneath the skin, strips of fatty bacon had been inserted. And finally, the whole lot was preserved in a lard concoction of rosé wine, black and white pepper corns, garlic, thyme and sage. It, too, had spent hours cooking slowly in the Roman black ovens of Blosseau. The venison will be served with a farofa of cooked casava and cornflower, mixed with onions, garlic and venison sausage, toasted until golden brown in butter.

The final and most exotic dish to make its appearance on tonight's menu is a favourite of Filipe's – vampire fish, or for the more civilised among us, the European Lamprey.

These are eel-like fish that migrate from the sea and swim up rivers such as the Gironde in Bordeaux and the Douro in Portugal, where they are caught and find their way into the cuisine of the coastal peoples.

Filipe's version is a nod to the Portuguese style lamprey arroz, served on a bed of rice, but here cooked in the French style, à la Bordelaise.

Lampreys are extremely slimy, making them difficult to work with, so Filipe needs to quickly blanche the long bodies in boiling water for a few seconds, to remove the slippery coating. Next, he hangs them by the tails from spikes so that the blood can be drained. Then he slices the bodies longwise and squeezes out what blood remains by running his hand from top to bottom, a bit like milking a cow. He cuts the bronchial holes to help the process. There's a lot of blood, and this operation is a delicate one, but the blood will be used later to thicken the sauce, so he catches it in a bowl beneath their gruesome little heads.

De-blooding successfully achieved, he removes the guts and pulls out the long black cord that runs the length of the fish, making sure to get all of it, so as not to contaminate the dish. Only then does he cut off the head, pulling out the long cartilaginous backbone at the same time. He has plans to plate the heads alongside the dish for effect.

Now he slices the bodies into small rounds and places them into earthenware bowls where they are marinated in Bordeaux wine, along with crushed garlic, bay leaves, parsley, salt and pink lemon from Rio de Janeiro.

While this is happening, he chops onion and red pepper into a pan and fries this up with small cubes of ham and pepperoni. He deglazes the pan with a little lamprey marinade and adds the rest of the fish to the simmering mixture, then gradually adds the rest of the marinade and uses the blood to thicken up the sauce at the last minute. The dish is served on a bed of rice that has been cooked using some of the marinade from earlier for flavour.

In a twist that surprises even Francesc, Filipe saves the heads to be breaded and fried and served as garnish, or for anyone brave enough to eat them.

Suddenly Filipe notices that a young boy has snuck into the kitchen and has been watching the preparation of the Lampreys with a singular fascination. He stops mid plate and beckons the boy over.

"Are these the vampire fish?" the young boy asks in an excited, breathless voice. "Madame la Boar said there would be vampire fish. I've never seen one before. Can I see one now? Do they bite? I'm going to be a famous scientist one day, so I make it my business to understand all strange things. Can I ask you a question?"

Filipe amusedly nods his head in the affirmative. There is a little of his younger self in the boy.

"Do they eat the blood of other fish? Is that why they're called vampire fish? Can I see their teeth?"

Filipe laughs. The boy certainly is a curious fellow. "Yes, they suck the blood of other fish by attaching themselves with their mouths. But they're not dangerous to humans. Do you want to see?"

Thoughts and words tumble out of the boy in a torrent. "Yes, please. Forgive my curiosity. As I said I am going to be a scientist and I read a book about the Nile River where they said that they found some clay pots with dried lamprey in them, and they thought that the lampreys could even eat the blood of the Nile Perch, the biggest fish in the whole of Egypt. Imagine studying a fish that was captured four-thousand years ago."

Francesc and Filipe look at each other. "Reminds one of someone else, eh?" says Francesc.

The boy continues, "I know another story about Lampreys. Do you want to hear it?"

Before either of the chefs can answer, the boy launches into his story. "One day the emperor Augustus was visiting his friend Vedius Pollio, an especially cruel man, known for executing those who displeased him by feeding them to his vampire fish. Well, on this occasion, Pollio became annoyed with a slave who had broken a goblet, and ordered the man to be thrown into the pond where the vampire fish lived.

Augustus, being a gentler man than his host, stopped the gruesome activity, and even went so far as to break all of Pollio's other valuable goblets as a sign of his displeasure. He even demolished Pollio's mansion."

The boy pauses for a moment, while Francesc and Filipe look at him in astonishment.

The boy waits a beat, and then continues, "Do you think they ate the vampire fish afterwards?"

With that they all burst into laughter. "What's your name?" asks Filipe.

"I apologise to the gentlemen for forgetting my good manners. The curiosity within me is greater than the etiquette our society asks. My name is Jean-François Champollion."

Suddenly Mme la Boar appears as if magically transported from another dimension. "Young man, there you are." Filipe flinches imperceptivity. She could just as well be referring to him when she says young man. "Where have you been, Jean-François? One moment you were in the library where I left you, and now you are here. Oh dear…" she turns her attention to the two chefs. "I apologise. I promised his brother, Jacques-Joseph Champollion, the older of these two child prodigies, that this one could come to the party if he behaved. And now look, his curiosity has gotten the better of him. All these questions that I never have the answers to… ha ha."

She begins to pull him back towards the stairs "Come on young man, let us leave the professionals to their work, vampire fish or no, the kitchen is a place for cooks, not scientists."

Filipe thinks she might not be altogether correct in her last statement. "Look, young Champollion, what do you say if I save you some of these heads in a glass jar and alcohol?"

The boy nods enthusiastically as the hostess propels him vigorously up the stairs.

*

* *

The mains are finally away and Francesc and Filipe go through a few final points with the kitchen and serving staff. Once everyone understands the rotation plan - the party will undoubtedly go on for a while yet - they uncork a bottle of red from Mme la Boar's reserves and sit down with some of the staff for a plate or two of the food they've worked so hard to create.

There is very little talking as they eat. Everyone agrees the food is spectacular.

Filipe gestures to Francesc with a sticky piece of crackling, "Perhaps my plan for peace between the peoples of the world is still possible, given our observations at this party."

The elder chef puts down his fork and ponders the concept. "Hmm, I had forgotten about your grand plan. Yes, perhaps the real test of such a thing would be to cook for two warring heads of state, or their fiery generals, and see whether they could forget their differences while facing each at the dining table. Even if we didn't manage to prevent all-out conflict, at the very least, we could put them in a good mood for a while." It's a semi-serious response to a highly speculative question. Certainly, there is no precedent in this regard.

The hypothesis, along with any examination of a potential experimental framework, is left hanging like so much steam in the air as Mme la Boar makes another one of her exuberant entrances. "Gentlemen, gentlemen, *mon dieu*, you have outdone yourselves. Between the confirmation of General Napoleon's advancement and the excitement of your food, I am at a loss. The compliments flowed like wine. The wine flowed like the compliments. I have never heard such praise for the food, ever, in this house. Congratulations. I could have died for the roast pork, and as for the venison with its marvellous farofa accompaniment … heavenly.

"The clergy of course went straight for the fish, although I must admit, the sight of the Lamprey heads caused them to cross themselves. Ha ha ha. The beastly little eels ended up being the toast of the whole banquet, nobody imagining such ugly little creatures could taste so divine.

"As expected, the younger guests flocked to the pheasant, while the older ones ate everything."

She seems to have come to the end of this round of effusive bubbling when she remembers something and hands Filipe an envelope, "Oh, and chef Filipe, young Champollion wrote you a note before he went to bed."

The note reads:

My dear chef Filipe,

My compliments for your outstanding work in the kitchen tonight. The lampreys were wonderfully scary and delicious at the same time. I confess that I never would have thought of eating such an animal, which I am sure would have been too sticky and slimy for human consumption without the benefit of your expertise. I believe that you are more than a chef; you are a scientist and an alchemist, and the kitchen is your laboratory. The dishes you cook are not just food, they are real gastronomic discoveries.

My compliments again, from one scientist to another.

Signed,

Jean-François Champollion, biologist and scientist extraordinaire.

Filipe is beaming from ear to ear. Francesc, meanwhile, cannot hide his pleasure and pride for his young protégé either, and gives Mme la Boar a knowing nod.

"Yes. You should be very pleased with yourselves my dears," says Mme la Boar, "now, some of the guests have asked to be introduced to the two geniuses responsible for tonight's dishes. I expect there are many parties and banquets in your future."

She beams from ear to ear, before becoming more business-like, "We will serve more champagne and drinks while the cold cuts and sweets are being refreshed in case anyone is still hungry. The party will go on well into the early morning hours. I suggest you chefs stay here tonight and get some sleep so that you have the energy for breakfast. By the way, what do you have planned for breakfast? By my calculations, we have utilised most of what you brought with you. Are we expecting an early morning delivery?"

Francesc lets Mme la Boar into part-two of their plan. "Well Madame, not exactly. You see, we have everything we need right here."

"Oh?"

"Yes indeed. You will notice that even though the guests enjoyed the food, there is still much left untouched. Rather than throw it all away, we will repurpose it and create something completely new, and I assure you, just as delicious."

The idea of such a thrifty and economical approach is a somewhat foreign concept in Mme la Boar's social circles, but she likes to think of herself as a progressive woman, and besides the two chefs have already proven that they are nothing if not inventive.

"Disguise it as a different meal? What a good idea. I approve! But perhaps we shall keep this little subterfuge to ourselves. Just what do you have planned?

"The left-over meats – the pork, deer, chicken, pheasant and sausage – we shall shred or cut into slices to be cooked with rice seasoned with paprika, chillies, coriander, leeks, wild garlic, saffron flowers and bay leaves. We'll call it a French Gypsy paella, and it will be the perfect breakfast after a night of carousing and partying."

"Well, you gentlemen are the experts; I shall leave the preparations up to you. So long as no-one thinks we have some kind of financial or food crisis. I look forward to it."

"Of course, you have our full discretion Madame. No one will be the wiser, I assure you."

*

**

Filipe and Francesc rise early, set out some croissants and coffee for those who are early risers, or more likely, have not yet gone to bed, and begin preparations on what is essentially part deux of the feast.

The paella goes out mid-morning and is met by a hungry and eager, if somewhat dishevelled crowd, who pronounce it one of the best meals they have ever had. Even one man, a Spaniard by birth, proclaims it to be heavenly, and begins singing some strange song.

Finally, the time comes for the two chefs to take their leave. They're in the process of loading their wagons with empty pots and pans when an officer appears with a note from General Bonaparte himself.

The general regrets that he has had to leave on urgent business without having had the chance to personally thank the chefs responsible for such an extraordinary banquet, but such is the life of a man whose service to his country is paramount. He hopes to rectify the discourtesy at a time in the future.

They thank the officer and depart with full hearts and a fuller purse, courtesy of Mme la Boar's treasurer. "Our gastronomic campaign has begun, Filipe," declares Francesc in a satisfied voice.

Reaching the restaurant, they are greeted at the door by Tereza, "Well, I'm glad you're back. It's not easy keeping up appearances here in this big place alone." They all laugh – this is exactly what they expected her to say.

Neither of them notices the man in black robes who has been following them from a discreet distance. Nor do they notice that he lingers just long enough to see that they are met at the door by a lone kitchen maid.

The kitchen at Chateau Blosseau.

CHAPTER 21

The cook with no name

"That which does not kill us makes us stronger."
Friedrich Nietzsche

A day or so after the big party at Chateau Blosseau, we find Francesc, Filipe and Tereza gathered around a small table in their restaurant kitchen, enjoying a breakfast of eggs, freshly baked bread, tea, and coffee that Dhortu assures them comes all the way from Brazil. They're almost touching heads as they all pore over the latest edition of the Nouvelles Extraordinaires, one of many gazettes focussing on the social comings and goings of a society on the brink of something extraordinary. "Ah. Here it is," says Francesc, and proceeds to read from the article:

Given the trials and tribulations that our beloved country has experienced more recently, it's not surprising that there are calls for a hero to rise; a man who will lead our embattled nation out of adversity, to reclaim our vaunted position in the world.

Two evenings ago, I had the honour of being invited to a feast at the chateau of Mme la Boar, a woman whose singular talent seems to be the bringing together of those most respected members of society in a setting matched only by the excellent quality of the cuisine. The pinnacle of the event was no doubt the attendance of a man whom this writer believes to be the very hero France has been crying out for – General Napoleon Bonaparte.

Tereza interjects before he can continue, "Does he mention the chefs by name?"

Francesc quickly scans the rest of the article and shakes his head.

"Well, the cheek of it. The party would have been a failure without you two."

Filipe puts a hand on Tereza's arm, "You're not wrong, Tereza, but in all honesty, who's interested in two chefs? Besides, we know people enjoyed the food, and that's the main thing."

Francesc nods his head in agreement, "Yes, I agree with Filipe. Of course, it hurts a little that we weren't mentioned, but the night was not for us. We will have our time. Soon people will know our names, and they will seek us out. Mark my words."

Tereza seems to be placated by this explanation, and adds cheekily, "Oh, so I suppose that will mean more parties for you while I'm stuck here at the restaurant alone, doing all the hard work? Very nice."

Filipe looks at her for a moment, not sure whether she's joking or serious, until she starts giggling at her own sauciness.

"As a matter of fact," says Francesc, winking at the girl "Filipe and I have decided that you are to accompany us to the next event. Starting today you are promoted to cook, and you will work alongside Filipe. We have great ambitions for you – perhaps you will become the first great female chef in France."

"Oh you…, I love you both," she blushes, and they all laugh again.

The rest of the day passes much like any other day. A steady stream of customers, as well as preparation for the many deliveries, keep them busy right up until the sun has cast its last rays and turned the clouds into pink puffs of candyfloss, before disappearing below the horizon for the night.

At supper, Tereza launches into a such a longwinded story about a friend who had fallen in love, that Francesc and Filipe are almost asleep at the table by the time she finishes. The day has tired them out. They say their goodnights and head for their respective rooms, where they all soon fall asleep, unaware of the turbulence brewing outside in the darkness.

*

* *

Political revolutions are like tides in a sea of discontent, with ideas pulled along by some invisible ideological force as it waxes and wanes. Often the imperceptible rising of the waters goes unnoticed until after they recede, leaving behind an accumulation of sticky churned up scum and other detritus.

On this night that scum comprises the confused remnants of a frustrated faction of some misguided radical group, whose revolution has turned inwards on themselves.

Three men in black clothing with even blacker hearts, break through the back door of Restaurant Petit, announcing themselves with a crash loud enough to wake the neighbourhood.

Jumping out of bed in fright, Tereza runs to Filipe's room and hugs him tightly.

Felipe, in just as much of a state of shock as Tereza, looks about wildly for a solution. He thinks immediately of Francesc's secret hiding place. He bundles Tereza into the concealed space and goes to Francesc's room. There's no sign of the older chef; he must have foolishly gone down to the kitchen to see what the commotion was all about.

Filipe descends to the kitchen, not knowing what he will find. It's not good. Francesc is on the floor, struggling with three scoundrels who are intent on tying him up.

"Filipe, NO!" he shouts. Get out of here. Run. Save yourself."

Even with their black cloaks, two of the three are recognisable to Filipe – the one clinging to Francesc's legs in an attempt to keep him on the ground is the guard who had confronted them at Mme la Boar's chateau on the day prior to the banquet. Next to him, tightening the rope around Francesc's neck is the same scowling Lieutenant Trusseau who had been so suspicious of the chefs as they went about their business in the kitchen. The third is a new face.

Clearly these men do not subscribe to the notion of spreading peace through a good meal. Or perhaps they did not have any of the food at the banquet. Or perhaps their hearts are just so filled with hatred and greed that there is no room for dessert.

Thoughts of trying to attack the men flash through Filipe's mind, but he is half their size and only one against three. He raises his arm in a moment of courage and shouts for them to stop. He's barely gotten the words out when the unknown man raises a pistol and fires at his face. A bright spark of light goes off at the side of his head, accompanied by vicious blow that hurls him into the canning cellar. Everything is suddenly black as Filipe falls backwards down the stairs. He lands with a thump but feels nothing.

*

* *

In the alleyway behind the restaurant kitchen, the pigeons are going about their usual morning activities. The noise of their busy cooing and scraping travels along the beams of sunlight which peep through the grimy outside window of the canning cellar and find Filipe's face. The young man opens his eyes with great difficulty and touches the side of his head. His hair is matted, and the entire left side of his face is still sticky from where he's been lying in a pool of his own blood. This is probably what saved him; with that much blood, the killers likely assumed he was dead.

Aside from the throbbing headache he can feel a searing pain just above his left ear. The bullet must have grazed his head without breaking the skull. A slight difference in the trajectory, and death would have been inevitable. But he's not dead. He's alive and …

He can't remember where he is. Or who he is. The more he tries to focus on the reason for his predicament, the cloudier things become. The shock of being shot in the head has wiped his memory.

He drags himself to his feet and staggers towards the stairs. The open cellar door is a yellow square somewhere above him. Like a moth to a flame, he climbs towards it.

In the kitchen above, he discovers a body lying on the floor. Does he know this person? It feels like he should. There's affection toward this man but he doesn't know why. Flashes of memory flood his brain. A man wearing an apron. A woman picking mushrooms in a field with a small boy. Who is the woman? Is the boy him?

Then more flashes of an old man teaching him how to shoot a rifle. The man smiles as a bullet from the gun shatters a small bottle. The old man's face changes. Now it's full of scars. The man is sitting in a wagon, entering a tunnel. Shouts echoing. Gunshots.

It's too much, the throbbing pain returns with a vengeance. Where am I? Who am I?

Through the broken kitchen door, he can see people running past. The noise from outside is overwhelming. He retreats into the relative quiet of the kitchen to get a better look at the man on the floor.

The light from the doorway goes dark for an instant as someone enters behind Filipe. He feels a hand on his shoulder, "Mon Dieu, you are full of blood. Are you ok? Is he dead? We cannot stay here. Come with me before they return. I can help you."

The man is strong. He lifts Filipe up and carries him to the sink where he wets a cloth and begins to rub the blood off the boy's face. There's a large gash where the lead grazed the skull, where the heat from the bullet has almost cauterized the wound. Filipe holds back his fear even as the rubbing of the cloth exacerbates the pain.

"We're going to help save the nation," says the man as he hoists Filipe over his shoulder and carries him into the street. Five or six blocks later they come to long line of men queueing in front of a military checkpoint. Queues apparently mean nothing to the man carrying Filipe; he walks directly to the front of the line, where he speaks to one of the soldiers.

The uniformed man looks Filipe up and down and sneers, "Another one. This one looks broken. What happened to his face?" He appears to think for a moment. "I'll pay half, take it or leave it."

The man carrying Filipe accepts two coins from the soldier and plonks Filipe down. "Good boy! I don't know what you did or why you're covered in blood, but your robes are from some respectable house...no matter, I don't care about your past...it's time to move on...your country needs you...today you join the army."

Filipe is too confused and disoriented to do anything but meld into the line of raggedy recruits and follow the swaying serpent of stinking bodies. The queue deposits him at the entrance to two military tents. In one tent are two men distributing uniforms. In the second, a man sits at a desk, writing in a large, leather-bound book. From time to time, he dips his pen in a small glass jar of ink before turning back to the book and continuing.

Filipe stands in front of the writing man for a few moments before the man acknowledges his presence.

"This is the queue to enlist. Have you come to enlist? What is your name, boy?"

Filipe remains silent. His brain seems not to be working very well.

"Your name. You must have a name."

Silence.

"No family name?"

Filipe stares dumbly at the man.

Without even a hint of irritation the man continues, "Another deaf and dumb one, eh?"

Filipe finally remembers how to speak, "I am not deaf sir. Nor am I dumb. I think I hit my head and I can't remember anything."

The man looks quizzically at Filipe for a moment. "You speak French, but you have an accent. Where do you come from boy?

"I really cannot say, sir. My mind is fuzzy."

"No name, no place of origin. No matter. Then you shall join the legion of the nameless. France needs bodies, not names. What about your profession. Can you do anything useful? What can I put in the book?"

The human body is a remarkable and complex thing, and the brain is the most complex component in this very complex machine. Filipe's brain, being the complex thing it is, decides to play a game with Filipe. Although his own name and anything else useful about who he is remains hidden in the mists of his mind, Filipe suddenly remembers something."

"I think I am a cook, sir. I remember being in a kitchen with food. Yes, I know how to cook."

'Well, well, well. A part of your memory returns. Good, the queue grows long because of your lack of remembering. I shall write here that you are the cook with no name. The army needs more good cooks, our food is rubbish. Perhaps you will change this, ha ha." The men in the tent look up from their piles of uniforms and laugh, too.

"Now go. But if you do remember your name, return here and we'll do things the right way. Either way, it makes no difference to me. Most recruits come from nowhere and will end up no place. The army will be your home from now on. And you shall have no other name than Cook.

Filipe joins the legion of the nameless.

CHAPTER 22

Military service

"If you've seen one, you've seen them all."
Margot Robert

The men in the Quartermaster's tent eyeball Filipe, measuring him up for a uniform and chef's whites. They hand him a small backpack and a rolled-up blanket and show him how everything fits together. "Best you take good care of those uniforms, we shan't be giving you another set. Now get fitted for boots over there and then visit the equipment and weapons tents to be kitted out."

Filipe does as they say without resistance. His head still aches, and even using his eyes seems to hurt. He goes from tent to tent, collecting gear as he goes. Groundsheet. Mug and canteen. Mess kit. Boot polish. Toiletries. When he finally gets to the weapons tent, a soldier issues him with a set of short swords to be worn at his waist.

"Cooks don't need guns; you will be content with your knives," says one.

"And forks," adds the other, as they both laugh.

"Clean up and get dressed. And go report to the head chef in the infantry kitchen."

"Sir, where is the kitchen?"

"Go forward in that direction and you will find your new squad."

*

* *

Filipe gets as far as a large tent where several men in various stages of undress are washing themselves in large basins and tin baths. No-one seems to mind when a fearless woman, carrying a large urn of hot water and followed by a group of dirty children, barges into their midst.

"Carry on gentlemen. If you've seen one, you've seen them all," she shouts jovially. The men laugh and carry on.

"You there," the woman spots Filipe, "come and look at me." She hands the boy a cloth. "Dear me. The war hasn't even started and this one is already injured. What on earth happened to you?" She turns him around and starts to dab at the wound above his ear.

"I think I was in an accident. I can't remember. I'm getting better now. I'm looking for the kitchen tent. I have to report to the head chef."

"Oh… what a surprise. We have a cook here. Will you be improving the dreadful food they serve us?" This brings a chuckle from the men. "Well, when you're done cleaning yourself up and changed out of those dirty clothes, I will take you to meet our head chef." She says the last two words with more than a soupçon of sarcasm. "Anyway, my name is Margot Robert. What's your name?"

"Madame, to be honest, I hit my head. I can't remember anything. Not even my own name. The only thing I know at the moment is that I think I like to cook."

"I had an uncle who hit his head once, and he didn't remember anything either. Or maybe it was the drink."

"Did he recover his memory?"

"Oh, no. He went crazy and died," she quickly adds, giving him a wink, "but you're young. I'm sure you will be fine."

The men laugh again. It's clear that they are enjoying this conversation a lot more than Filipe is.

Margot Robert certainly is a character with a sense of humour as vigorous as she is. A large, ample bosomed specimen, whose powerful forearms have been sculpted by a lifetime of hefting giant cooking pots, wringing laundry and wrangling children, and which would be equally at home in an arm-wrestling contest. Despite her stout construction, she moves with a surprising nimbleness, her buttocks bouncing up and down under her skirt like two small animals trying to escape a drowning-sack, propelling her across the ground as though they were filled with some lighter-than-air-gas.

Her round face is pretty to look at, with doe-eyes framed by impossibly long lashes, and a wide, Chaucerian gap-toothed smile.

By the way the men interact with her, she's clearly a mother figure for the entire regiment.

She helps Filipe figure out the multitude of buttons on his uniform, shows him where to stow the rest of his kit and brings him to the kitchen tent where she introduces him to the gang.

The "gang" comprises eight cooks in uniform, six civilian woman kitchen-helpers, and to Filipe's surprise, a gaggle of children, who he later learns are pickers, or foragers, whose job it is to forage for things like herbs, mushrooms and wild vegetables, as well as to trap small animals – anything for the pot, just as Filipe himself had done on his journey to France with his father. Filipe had never considered that anyone other than men were involved in an army, but here they were – pint-sized warriors of sorts, large as life and twice as boisterous.

In charge of this merry gang is the chef de cuisine, Lieutenant Guion Touchot, a somewhat nervous and insecure man, who wastes no time reminding Filipe of his place in the pecking order.

"Is this the boy who doesn't know his own name? I wonder if you know how to fry an egg. Well, regardless, we need someone who can chop potatoes and wash pots. Keep quiet and do as you're told, and we shall get on fine."

The women are whispering among themselves and staring at the ugly scar above the boy-who-lost-his-memory's right ear as though he's a fairground curiosity. Margot shushes them with a gesture, "Where are your manners, it could happen to anyone."

Filipe sighs and shakes his head. The headache still lingers.

One woman offers him a chunk of bread and a dried sausage. "Eat. You look hungry. We'll talk after."

Filipe realises he is indeed hungry and gobbles the food down with a cup of tea that someone thrusts into his hand. He addresses the boss.

"Sir, do we cook for the entire army?"

"I've never been asked that before. What do you think boy? Do you think fifteen people could cook for an entire army? Of course not. We cook for the Sixth Infantry. And that is enough, believe you me."

Looking out over the sprawling camp, Filipe can't even begin to imagine cooking for an entire army. Feeling suddenly faint, he sits down against a log and falls asleep.

The chef starts to say something, but Margot interrupts him, "Leave him be, he's been through his own war. I'll show him the ropes when he wakes up."

Touchot nods and goes about his business.

* * *

It's morning the next day. Or possibly the day after that. Filipe has no way of guessing. All he knows is that he's been rudely awakened by the noise of a wagon bouncing through a pothole. The sound of horses and clamouring voices brings him to the present.

The army is readying itself to move. If Filipe were a giant, he might look down upon the column of soldiers and be reminded of army ants carrying their materials along to some unknown, collective destination.

The regiment decamps and sets off on the long march towards Italy. Hours and hours go by, who can say how many kilometres they cover. Eventually a rider appears and blows a trumpet signalling that they should stop and make camp.

Filipe and the kitchen crew light a fire and begin to reconstruct their kitchen. They bring the carts around into a shallow, wide horseshoe shape facing the fire. Tents are erected. Tables go up. Pots and pans are unpacked. By the time they have established their territory, the sun has disappeared below the horizon. The light of the burning fire throws a warm glow onto the kitchen encampment making it look curiously inviting. Crackling and spitting logs add their voice to the hubbub of soldiers going about their various tasks.

The moment is interrupted by a shout, "Hear ye, hear ye, upon the orders of General Bonaparte…"

Touchot and the kitchen staff immediately stop what they're doing to listen.

Bonaparte. Filipe has heard that name before. Where? He can't remember, so he just turns his attention toward the messenger.

"By order of the General: I hereby give you new rules governing the deployment of staff and rations in the kitchens.

"Rule the first, as to the allocation of bread, which much not exceed twenty-four ounces per man, per day. Although this might seem generous now, we will need to take care to ration the flour so that it may be evenly distributed during the campaign.

"Rule the second, every soldier is to be given half a pound of meat per day, plus an ounce of rice or two ounces of beans or peas or lentils, along with a pint of wine, a gill of cognac and half a gill of vinegar.

"Rule the third, the cooks are to produce, daily, the traditional dumplings, made of flour, salt and water, which they will cook either baked over an open fire or mixed with stew. Soldiers shall be served no more or less than two per day.

"Rule the fourth, the cooks shall produce stews and other dishes utilising whatsoever the scouts, hunters, and child collectors are able to gather along the way.

"These terms are specifically established for the chefs of the rank and file of army battalions, that they are responsible for the planning, cooking, and provisioning of their kitchens. Chefs shall furthermore be prudent in their use of provisions, conserving the food belonging to the French Army where and when they can.

"It is the final responsibility of the chefs, under pain of death, that they, and their colleagues, refrain from availing themselves of the provender that has been earmarked for the officers of the General's army."

With that, the soldier rolls up his scroll and rides off on his horse.

Felipe is quiet. So, apparently there are two standards — one for the men and quite another for the officers. His experience in the kitchen tells him that there are difficult times ahead and if they aren't careful, they might well go hungry. Hopefully the scouts and the child-gatherers will be able to keep up with the inevitable demand.

Lieutenant Guion Touchot watches him intently. Could it be that the boy is analysing the ration situation? Surely, he is too young. Let's see how he does in practice; he thinks to himself.

"Filipe, you take two soldiers and go to the wagons for flour, salt and yeast. You will be making bread for the troops tonight. Try not to break the sacks when you lift them."

Then, without waiting for a response he barks further orders to a group of young soldiers standing nearby. "You two, unload the bricks from the kiln wagon and I will help you assemble the ovens; and you lot, over there, go out and search for whatever firewood you can find, supper is not going to cook itself."

Filipe is impressed. The ovens are of a construction that allows them to be dissembled for transport and then reassembled again at their destination. What seemed chaotic at first now appears to come together with remarkable efficiency. Was superior logistics the secret to the Bonaparte's success? What other surprises were in store for the young chef?

Chef Touchot splits the group into two cohorts. Himself in charge of one team and by careful design, Filipe overseeing the other. After making sure that his own preparations are satisfactorily underway, he wanders over to see how team Filipe is doing, half expecting them not even to have started. To his surprise, not only have they started, but the small dumplings and loaves that have been laid out in the baking trays are all perfectly symmetrical in size and shape. What's more, the boy chef seems to be giving a masterclass to his assistants.

Muttering under his breath, Touchot returns to his own station. Harumph! Let's see what happens when they come out of the ovens. Our tastebuds shall tell the real tale.

The moment of truth arrives. The head chef selects a dumpling from his own team and bites into it. Good. Then, with an almost child-like curiosity, he takes one from Filipe's team and does the same. A strange look registers on his face. He reaches for another one.

The chefs all look on in anticipation.

Touchot's face breaks out into a wide grin, "Mon Dieu how did you do this?"

He turns his attention to the larger loaves, "Let us now taste the bread."

Same thing.

All eyes look on expectantly. He's quiet for a moment, apparently thinking about what to do next. Finally, he speaks, "If you are all waiting for a verdict, here it is. I cannot tell a lie. These dumplings and bread are delicious." He turns to Filipe, "Congratulations. You have a talent for cooking that I never doubted from the first time I met you. Starting today we will work side-by-side, and in time, hopefully, you will remember where this talent comes from. Until then, you will cook with me.

Images and flashes of a happy kitchen float through the young chef's head; a smiling woman in a kitchen somewhere, his mother? He longs to remember properly and perhaps in time he will. Touchot has mentioned something about the Kingdoms of Italy. He thinks he has a connection to Italy. He's not sure.

That night, asleep in his tent, Filipe suddenly awakes. He remembers everything. He knows who he is.

I am Felipe, an Italian with a French father.

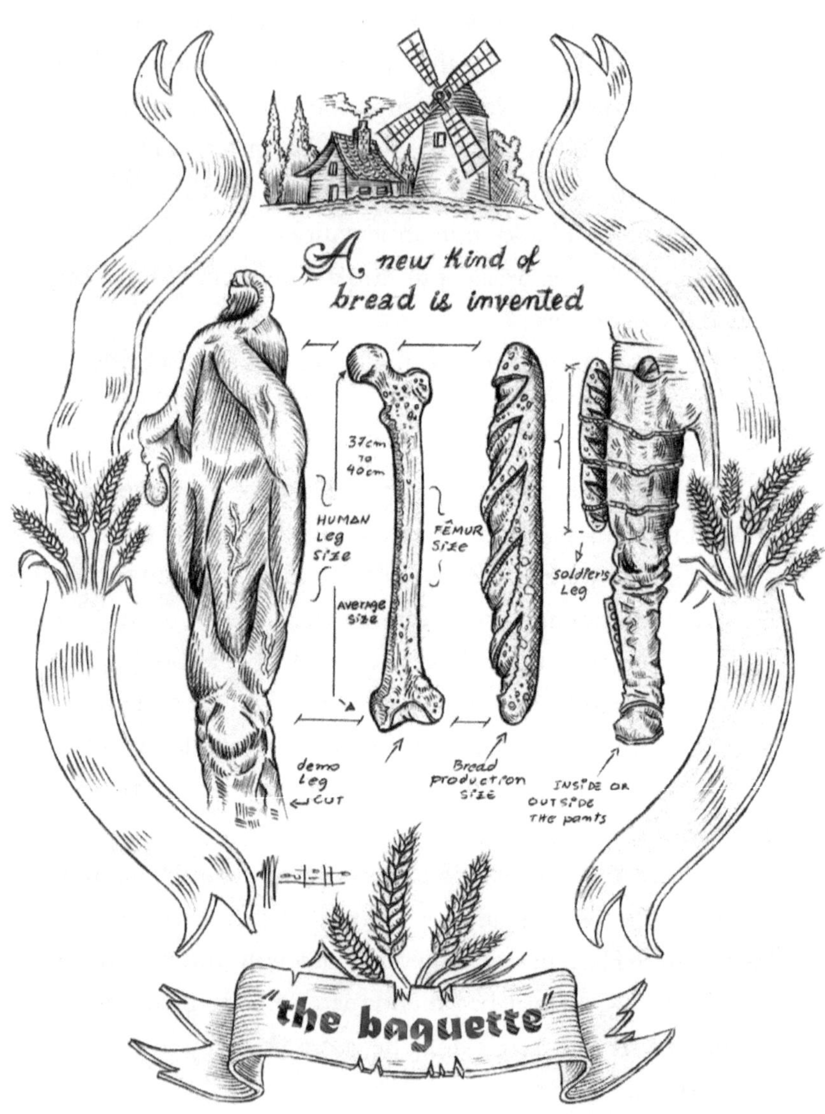

A new bread format for soldiers, thus the baguette was born.

CHAPTER 23

The chef of chefs

"An army marches on its stomach."
Napoleon

In many cases amnesia is a temporary disorder, lasting from a few seconds to a few hours, to a few days. Of course, the condition can persist, depending on the severity of its cause. In Filipe's case the cause was the traumatic shock of being shot in the head, an event that was quite possibly further exacerbated by falling down the stairs immediately thereafter. Fortunately, the damage to Filipe's hippocampus (scientists tell us this the area of the brain responsible for memories) was not permanent. Indeed, the damage might have been much worse, leaving him without part of his memory forever, but as it was, he was healing fast, perhaps due to his young age, or simply because as a chef, living with Francesc and Tereza, his body had benefited from a rich diet of whole grains, nuts, pork, yeast and legumes that were high in thiamine.

Now the memories come flooding back in an overwhelming and confused jumble. He remembers seeing his friend and mentor, Francesc, lying motionless on the floor. Was he dead? And what of Tereza? These recollections leave him bewildered and depressed. What a cruel place the world could be.

But there is something else that returns along with his memory. Napoleon's army is marching toward Italy, his place of birth. A secret that only Francesc had known. He cannot tell anyone of his true heritage. He remembers Francesc's words, Felipe, let me talk to that one, don't open your mouth so he doesn't hear your Piedmontese accent.

His late father had said something similar, Felipe, do not let anyone know that you were born in an Italian region, the world is at war, and it is not good for anyone to know your true roots.

It seemed that the two older men had somehow predicted the world would become a battleground, where brother would fight brother just as Cain and Able had done in the bible.

The danger was that his own colleagues would become his enemies. No, he must not let on. His must pretend that he still cannot remember anything of his own background. He is a cook with no name, and that is all anyone needs to know about him.

*

* *

Over time, his colleagues in the field kitchen grow quite fond of the young chef who is never too busy to lend a helping hand to the kitchen girls to clean vegetables, chop onions or prepare ingredients for the other chefs. He makes them laugh with his funny stories and imitations of the voices and mannerisms of some of the officers. Margot has even started referring to him as her son, laughing at his strange diversions and curious manner.

The other cooks begin to look up to him as he shows them different techniques for preparing and cooking. The foraging children bring him rabbits, pheasants, truffles, fish, potatoes, wild garlic and whatever they can find along the way to please him. Whenever there's spare time, Filipe joins them to play, or to kick a cloth ball to each other in a merry circle.

Even grumpy Lieutenant Guion Touchot has grown to like the boy who arrived in his territory and stole the show. Following the fiasco of their first cook-off, the lieutenant had resolved to mitigate his tone, and has even stopped making jokes about Filipe's memory and his being unable to remember how to boil an egg. Truth be told, Touchot has come to admire Filipe's talent.

Soon everyone has started to notice improvements in the quality of food coming out of the kitchen. A great number of soldiers have started to appear at the kitchen tent to compliment the chefs on their cooking and reminisce about how the food reminds them of home.

A rising tide raises all boats, as the saying goes, and one morning, Lieutenant Touchot, his own confidence raised by the collective accomplishments of his team, and perhaps struck by a sudden creative rush of blood to the head, even ventures so far as to invent a new kind of bread to replace the unpopular pain égalité that has been the staple since the revolution. His new creation is a long, thin loaf that soldiers can carry more easily in their arms, or even stuffed into their trouser legs, if necessary.

The new loaves are an instant success and are affectionately called baguettes by the soldiers, after the French word for "baton".

*

* *

Napoleon was an astute man. An avid reader who constantly sought out knowledge in the great stories of history – Julius Caesar, Hannibal, Nebuchadnezzar. He thought that by understanding their tactics he, too, might rise to be one of the world's great leaders.

It was not just the victories that interested Napoleon, but the failures and defeats as well. Napoleon theorised that one of the biggest causes of failure in battle was because the generals only paid attention to their officers, ignoring the rank and file who knew the reality on the ground. He resolved not to make this same mistake and actively sought out the opinions of his men, as he put it, a duty to know the minds of the soldiers. He developed a network of informants who kept him abreast of the mood among the fighting corps.

It is in a meeting with such an informant that Napoleon learns of a most popular new invention, the baguette. He is impressed, but this is not the only good news. According to the intel he is receiving, the general morale of the sixth battalion is higher than that of the other battle battalions, and the direct result, he is curiously informed, of a marked improvement in the food the soldiers are eating.

"Bring me the men responsible," he orders, "I would speak with them. In an army it is necessary to seek out those who inspire others."

The General's aide-de-camp, first lieutenant du Bois, doesn't need to be told where to find the answer. He rides immediately for Touchot's field kitchen. On the way, he ponders how best to tell Napoleon that the person responsible for all of this is a young man who doesn't even know his own name. This simple answer doesn't seem to be a feasible one for a man as practical as Bonaparte. How could a person with no name even enlist? It was a dilemma. The best course of action would be to talk to Guion Touchot himself and bring him and the boy back to meet Napoleon.

Lieutenant Touchot puffs himself up like a peacock in the imperial gardens as he receives the news that he is to report to the great General, a man who, even after all his years in the army, he has never met. A pang of jealousy pings him momentarily; the real reason for all of this is not himself, after all, but a boy who can't even remember his own name. No, he puts the thought out of his mind. Although the boy is several years his junior, they're equals in the kitchen. And that's the way it should be.

"Call the Nameless One, tell him to get ready quickly. We're going to meet the big boss."

The three arrive at Napoleon's big tent. The aide de camp remains outside talking to some soldiers while Guion and Filipe are ushered inside by a fearsome looking dragoon guard. The interior of the tent is littered with maps. An understanding of cartography is a basic requirement for a great strategist, thinks Filipe. They pass through a curtain and the guard announces them. "The two men from the Sixth are here General." Napoleon stands among piles of books and more charts like the one in the first chamber. An avid reader indeed, thinks Filipe to himself. The stories must be true.

Napoleon washes his hands in a basin and turns to face the chefs who are at this juncture doing their best impression of two meerkats – standing straight up, eyes wide with anticipation. The General looks them up and down and approaches them, stockinged feet silent on the Persian rugs spread across the floor of the tent.

"Bonjour gentlemen. Am I addressing the men responsible for changing the shape of my soldiers' bread and feeding my Sixth Regiment? Tell me this – what is the secret to your success? Are you increasing the rations in defiance of my orders?" He knows the premise of this last question is untrue, but he liked to test the mettle of his soldiers.

"General, I ask permission to speak freely," Lieutenant Guion says with a reserved firmness.

Napoleon nods in agreement. "Speak up."

"With respect, General, I am Lieutenant Guion Touchot, head of the food supply section of the Sixth Battalion. Telling the purest truth, we have not increased the portions for any soldier or other person. The measurements remain the same as stipulated by the General himself, not an ounce more or less. Last month we were able to send leftover flour to the Seventh Battalion since our provisions grow beyond out needs thanks to our collections and accurate apportioning system…"

Napoleon interjects, "Stop, please. I already know the truth of this. I wanted to hear it from the horse's mouth, so to speak. Continue."

Guion breathes a sigh of relief as a bead of sweat runs down his temple. Napoleon's eyes follow the drop as if it were a cannonball as it falls to the carpet but says nothing.

"I am the man responsible for the new loaves, and as you can see, the baguette is a more efficient shape. But the person really responsible for the improvement in the cuisine is this young man standing next to me. He was born with a divine talent. He is the one who has shown us how to measure the provisions correctly so that there is no wastage. And he is also the one who directs the foraging children to find the best wild ingredients."

"I admire your honesty lieutenant; a lesser man might have wanted the credit for himself. As to your baguettes, I have ordered all bakers to follow your configuration. Soon all the regiments will adopt this new way of doing things."

Filipe is thinking that the General is not as short as some gazettes portray him to be. In fact, here in the confines of the tent, he seems bigger than most. He shuffles and looks at the floor.

Napoleon scrutinises Filipe for a moment and says, "Identify yourself soldier, and tell me how you manage to cook with such elan."

"Sir, General…I don't want to sound like a boiled plum. Please try to understand that in the days before joining the army I had a terrible accident to the head. As a result, I cannot remember anything. Not my own name, nor those of my family members, or even if I had a family. The field kitchen is my family now. The only thing I know is that I am a cook."

Napoleon's answer surprises him, "…yes indeed, so you are the cook with no name. You look familiar to me. Perhaps we shall come to know your name in time. Tell me, how is it that you manage your kitchen so much better than others?"

"In truth I owe everything to my colleagues; Lieutenant Touchot is a good leader, and the cooks are more than capable. All the women of the camp are helpful and attentive to our work, and the children-collectors are of great use. As for talent, I can only say that I cook with my soul, it is who I am."

"A tasty story," says the General, "I like men who are eloquent and passionate about their mission. We will get on very well, you and I, I think. I have plans for you."

Both chefs give their best impressions of listening closely.

"It boils down to this; every resource is precious in times of war. And you, gentlemen are extremely precious resources. If I were an extravagant man, I would immediately install you as cooks in my own personal kitchen without batting an eye, as I am sure many of my foolish officers would do. And perhaps I will still do so in the future. But no. For now, I am appointing you as my food ambassadors. You shall go forth among the battalions and regiments and teach your techniques to the other chefs and kitchens. How to forage. How to store. How to conserve. How to dice. How to stew. Even how to boil an egg if it becomes necessary. You are my secret weapons. An army marches on its stomach, and you will ensure that my army's stomach is full and happy."

Filipe smiles a quiet inward smile. Perhaps his plan for world peace through good food was not impossible after all. Not in so many words, but Napoleon has certainly insinuated that he expects the improvement in cuisine to cause an improvement in morale. If nothing, this is a step in the right direction.

The General continues in a more serious tone, "We must be serious for a moment. I'm sure I'm not mistaken in assuming you gentlemen have ascertained the true circumstances of our predicament. Our food supplies are woefully insufficient to last us as we enter enemy territory. You must continue to do what you can do to keep the troops happy with your systems of foraging and food storage. Stretch the budget, as the politicians like to say. I, nay, the entire France, is relying on you.

"Now onto another matter. As recognition of your service, I am promoting both of you, effective immediately."

A look passes unnoticed between the two chefs. Napoleon's praise is both a blessing and a curse. With higher rank came more money. But now their mission would be bigger. Napoleon was right, the food was far from sufficient, and they have somehow been made responsible for the wellbeing of the entire army. Filipe gulps, almost audibly. The moment is certainly not lost on the young chef.

The great General has moved on from the subject of insufficient rations, "Let me inspire your efforts with a story about a great feast that I had the pleasure of attending recently. Now, I am more gourmand than gourmet, I gobble chicken with my hands, and prefer fatty foods and thick broths, but this feast … well, I should say, I have never experienced quite anything like it.

"As I say, there was a banquet, in celebration of my recent promotion to Major General, hosted by an old friend, Mme la Boar. The hostess served an array of dishes as formidable as France herself, famously presented by two Parisian chefs. Though I cannot remember the names of the chefs – I was called away by the obligations of war before I got to meet them – the food is something I shall never forget.

"There was an ornate pheasant dish, garnished with a centrepiece of its own feathers, reminiscent of the curlicues in the palaces and fine houses, platters piled high with great chunks of pork crackling, the tenderest venison and an exquisite brandade of cod, but there was one dish that stood out among the rest. A dish made from a most strange fish, an eel from the estuaries of France, so they tell me. The chefs had played a trick on the diners by serving the heads alongside the flesh – fearsome little faces that both taunted and dared the guests some closer. Some called them vampire fish.

"I confess, being a man of simple tastes, I did not partake of this extravaganza, but settled for a simpler, Asian-inspired dish of noodles and tamarind…"

Here the General stops mid-sentence and seems to be reminiscing about something, "Where was I? A simple Asian dish among the overindulgent extravagance of the French fare. Yes, these two chefs were unafraid to embrace the flavours of cultures not our own. I was reminded of a story I once read about the Japanese Samurai, one in particular by the name of Nobunga, whose embrace of foreign technology gave him a distinct advantage in battle in a battle at a place called Nagashino.

"In this great Japanese legend, the story begins some years prior in the Portuguese enclave of Macao, with a Portuguese ship, headed up the coast toward Shanghai. The ship is blown off course by a giant typhoon and is eventually wrecked on the coast of Japan. The survivors are rescued by a clan of Samurai, who also discover a powerful weapon among the Portuguese cargo – the flintlock rifle.

"But the flintlock, as powerful as it was, had its shortcomings. It disgorged a great deal of smoke and noise, making it hard to conceal one's position. Moreover, the weapon was cumbersome to reload, taking up to a minute to do so, even for skilled fusiliers.

"In the story of the famous battle of Nagashima, it is said that Nobunga's enemy, Katsuyori, having heard the first volley from the flintlocks, and being well aware of their shortcomings, sent in a second wave, hoping to overpower Nobunga's men before they could reload.

"Unbeknownst to the attackers, Nobunga had organised his men into alternating ranks, allowing one rank to fire their weapons as the other reloaded, facing off the enemy in an almost continuous volley of lead.

"Yes… embrace the unfamiliar…" Here Napoleon seems to lose his train of thought.

*

* *

Filipe is not sure quite what the moral of this story is, other than perhaps there are too many thoughts in the man's head. He's tempted to admit that he, Filipe, was one of the chefs at the great feast of La Boar; it's obvious that the food made an impression on the great General. But no, he decides not to reveal himself before he understands more of Napoleon's intent. There would be time enough. He resolves there and then that he needs to install himself somehow as chef in the officer's kitchen.

Napoleon regains his original mental track and comes back to the matter at hand. "Go forth and spread your expertise. Wars must be won quickly, else they create further problems like starvation and disease. You gentlemen must use your knowledge to thwart the first. The second we leave in the hands of God."

They leave the plush tent and return to the muddy reality that is an army on the march. Napoleon has placed a great responsibility onto the shoulders of his two chefs. War is immanent – it will be difficult to achieve their mission, if not impossible.

Napoleon is left sitting on a rustic couch contemplating whatever it is that generals contemplate in quiet moments alone. He wonders about the cook with no name. His manner is that of an educated person, not one who drinks too much and becomes indigent; not that of some poor unfortunate who melts his bones and his mind with grog and forgets his own name.

Filipe for his part is left with something far more important and fundamental from the encounter. He had undoubtedly touched the General with his cooking. But the General's bellicosity persists. The young chef swears on the memory of his mentor, chef Francesc Alain Petite, that he will find a way into Napoleon's heart via his stomach, and bring peace to the world through his cooking.

Filipe and the kitchen staff set for the front line.

CHAPTER 24

Haute cuisine

"The meaning of life is to find your gift.
The purpose of life is to give it away."
Pablo Picasso

Filipe wastes no time enlisting the help of Guion, Margot and the kitchen staff, along with the cleaning ladies and the foraging children, to create a more mobile and streamlined version of their travelling kitchen. The newly formed mini-platoon sets out on what amounts to a culinary greatest-hits tour of the front line – their goal being to bring whatever wisdom they can to the multitude of field kitchens that fuel the tens of thousands of stomachs on their relentless march toward glory.

What they discover is just about as far from what they expected to find as they could ever have imagined.

One of the main reasons for the unnecessary loss of provisions is not simply carelessness, but rather that many of the field chefs and their staff simply cannot not read or write, let alone compute rationing calculations.

Filipe's solution for this is to install a blackboard in each of the kitchens. On it, for the benefit of those who can understand written language and numbers – and hopefully transfer this knowledge verbally to others – he writes the basics of their everyday meal plans. Measurements for flour, water, yeast, salt; approximate weights of protein per man (a big chicken could satisfy four men, for example). Even such simple modifications would prove to have an immediate, and huge, impact.

Guion and Margot, between the two of them, dream up the idea for putting together a sort of cookery class for making the most of their rations, aimed at those who do not have even a basic understanding of mathematics. Not for nothing, but the classes attract a good deal more women than men. Either the men are too proud to admit they don't know something, or the women simply have had less access to traditional learning and therefore see it as something more valuable than the men do.

Margot shows her students how to make three markings with a knife on the inside of their tin cups to represent standard measurements:

Top line - whole portion.

Line halfway up - half portion.

Bottom line ¼ portion.

Simple solutions that would prove to be powerful in their application.

Very quickly, the students start to come up with their own ideas, making similar markings inside their large pots and cauldrons and laughingly telling each other that this recipe calls for ½ a pot, or that recipe ¼ of a cup.

Filipe and Guion make a point of talking not just with the kitchen staff, but also with the troops themselves. On one such occasion they discover that very few of the soldiers still have their own teeth. The lucky ones have rudimentary dentures fashioned from hippopotamus or walrus ivory. Some of the more well-off have dentures made from actual human teeth fixed to an ivory base. This made the hard, long-lasting biscuits that the kitchens produced rather unpopular, since even those with teeth struggled to chew them properly.

Filipe makes suggestions for alternatives that will be easier to palate.

They spend time with the foraging children from the various camps they visit, teaching them which mushrooms can be eaten, and which not, how to recognise the many and varied wild herbs that grow in abundance throughout the landscape - if only one knew where to look - and how to trap hares and pheasants, with a caution that they leave the larger animals, such as deer and boars – especially! –to the soldiers.

A month goes by, and word reaches them that Napoleon is pleased. The great General has been informed that the chefs have been being successful in their mission. More important than that, though, the soldiers are expressing their appreciation. Everyone is enjoying the new cooking.

On the heels of this success, Filipe is summoned. He is to leave the Sixth Battalion and report to the officer's mess. This brings mixed feelings; on the one hand he'll miss the kitchen family who took him in even without a name. On the other, this is precisely what he wants – to be closer to Napoleon.

As he goes through the motions of saying goodbye to his friends, he can't help thinking of his old friend and mentor, Francesc. He and Francesc had had a singular goal, to make people happy through food. And in pursuit of this goal, they had raised the state of their art to a place that transcended mere cooking. It was haute cuisine, thought Filipe. He thinks back to a time before he met Francesc, when he cooked without any real purpose other than to cook. Now the haute stood for a higher purpose.

He dwells on a conversation he'd had with Francesc about finding inner peace through food and meditation. How Francesc, instead of ridiculing his grand ideas of bringing peace through food, had encouraged him to explore the thought further.

Filipe remembers his words at the time, "Happy men don't fight and kill each other; full stomachs do not leap at each other's throats. Nobody has ever killed anybody else while eating a mouthful of cake."

Filipe doesn't know whether such ideals are yet achievable, but he does know that he is going to get to test his grand theory on one of Europe's great warmongers.

*

* *

Filipe's new colleagues in the officer's kitchen are passable chefs at best. Here are not the great minds who might make their names in the culinary world by codifying cuisine into something pure; nor are these men the likes of Sylvain Bailly and the other Paris contemporaries of Francesc. Rather, these are unctuous, scheming men, ever seeking the praise of the officers they cook for, quick to take offence of their underlings. And on more than one occasion, taking credit for Filipe's cooking.

Politicians. Not cooks, thinks Filipe. He keeps his head down and conducts himself in a reserved manner, deftly manoeuvring himself around their shenanigans, waiting for his chance to shine.

Napoleon's army is almost at the Italian border. The landscape reminds him of the crossing he made with his father and old Luc at what now seems a long, long time ago. Filipe is chewing over these thoughts when word comes down that Napoleon is hosting a dinner for all his senior officers, and that they, the chefs of the officer's mess, are expected to produce something worthy of the occasion. What is the great General up to? Filipe thinks to himself. Was the cunning old fox planning to discuss strategy before finally crossing into Italy?

These are questions Filipe cannot answer, but the situation does present Filipe with an opportunity. He puts his plan into motion. He will create a meal in secret with his old colleagues back at the Sixth and serve it at the dinner to show what he can do.

Filipe enlists the help of the foraging children in his plan. They smuggle white beans and potatoes out of the main stores. Pablo, a dog that they have adopted somewhere along the way, turns out to be quite the truffle hound, and is instrumental in locating a fine crop of the white truffles common in this part of the world.

True to form, the other chefs ignore Filipe, too busy and self-important to delegate even the simplest of dishes to the young cook. So, it's easy for him to slip away unnoticed and join Guion, Margot, and his erstwhile colleagues back at their field kitchen. Their dish is a white bean cream with warm cod salad, potatoes, and white truffles. Simple, elegant, and if Filipe has anything to say on the matter, delicious.

They cover the dish in cloth and make their way back to the officers' tent where Filipe's new colleagues are milling about in the disorganised fashion of schoolboys waiting for the headmaster, waiting to serve their crude menu. Filipe marches straight past them into the lion's den. He looks Napoleon directly in the eye, standing for a few moments, before speaking. "Gentlemen, in honour of this gathering, I have made a special dish that I would like you to try."

Napoleon, clearly oblivious to the Greek drama that is about to unfold before the audience of senior officers, answers, "Yes, and why not? That is your job after all, is it not? I mean, to cook, not to sew our breeches." The officers laugh at this witticism from their leader.

With that Filipe signals to Margot, who strides in on those fabulous buttocks of hers, and with a flourish worthy of a bullfighter, unveils the dish and places it on the table. Caught completely unaware, the chefs of the officer's mess shoot daggers of hate at Filipe.

But they, along with their petty attitudes, are of no consequence at this point in the proceedings. The aroma of

Filipe's food has filled the tent with its deliciousness, lifting the mood, like hot air entering Montgolfier's famous balloon. The officers attack the food with the same vigour they presumably bring to their endeavours on the battlefield, and for a time there is only the sound of forks rattling against porcelain and the odd smacking of lips. Then a murmur of appreciation rises. Napoleon looks toward the entrance to the tent where the other chefs stand awkwardly, shuffling their feet. A look passes across his face, as though the cogwheels of his mind have suddenly engaged. He addresses Filipe directly, "Lieutenant, you have surprised our palates – for the first time in a while, I might add – while your colleagues hide behind the curtains like Polonius," he gestures to the now thoroughly miserable bunch milling around at the entrance to the tent.

"No, it's now abundantly clear to me that your colleagues have stifled your talent out of jealousy, or spite, or perhaps just sheer stupidity." He addresses the chefs, "Gentlemen, the enemy is out there, not in here. Your own bitterness has done us all a great disservice. Fear and resentment have no place in my army. They are as a poisonous snake whose head we must cut off before they destroy a successful campaign."

Then he looks toward the chaplain, seated midway down the table, "Father, there's a good subject for your next sermon, do you not think. Condemn all envy and corruption. Love they neighbour and all that, eh? And speaking of love, tomorrow I shall go to Paris to marry my beloved Josephine."

He looks back at the chefs, "In my absence, take the good example that has been shown by this young chef tonight. He showed us courage. And that is what we shall need when we meet Italy on the battlefield. As I said, gentlemen, the enemy is out there, not in here."

The priest nods his assent, what else can he do? Napoleon indicates that the dinner is over, noting that Filipe has done well to put aside the black intentions of his colleagues, and congratulates him once again on a delicious meal.

In the days that follow, the men who had frustrated Filipe's efforts are given lashes and dismissed. Filipe once again becomes the centre of unwanted attention, although it must be said, far from negative. He hears the murmured comments about Napoleon being a righteous man, and he, Filipe being some kind of culinary genius. The grapevine is abuzz. Filipe ignores the whispers and focusses on his goal. And waits for Napoleon to return.

When the great General does return, barely a week later, he's in a warring mood. His absence has been so brief that many of the soldiers haven't even noticed he was gone. Before Filipe knows it, they are at war with the Piedmontese. He watches in horror as the people of his homeland come under attack. If there is any consolation to be had, Napoleon wants the war over and done with quickly, with minimal casualties on both sides, and more to point, before the Austrians can join the fray.

The fighting lasts two weeks before Napoleon declares victory.

The young chef is devastated. He wonders if his homeland will ever be the same again. He wonders if he, Filipe, will ever be the same again. Everywhere he looks there is death and destruction. Bodies dressed just as his grandfather used to dress, piled on top of one another. Dead horses, bloated, stinking, and covered in flies. Canons pointed in every direction other than that which would be useful. Splintered trees, burnt bushes, charred undergrowth. Mist mixes with the still smouldering ground, making it look like a scene straight out of hell.

Perhaps even more horrifying to Filipe, he sees the foraging children stripping the corpses of anything useful. Ghouls, straight out of hell, picking at the bones and sucking out the souls of the unlucky and the unrighteous.

It was hard to imagine that anyone was winning the war. To a very tired Filipe and his colleagues, the General's boundless ambition seems to know no limits. But there were enough small successes to keep the men believing.

Filipe is not like most of the other men, however. For one thing, he's gifted with a rare intelligence, and an appetite for books and reading that he satiates by the light of the dim oil lantern in his tent at night. Some of what he reads disturbs him.

It's not all peaches and cream in Paris. Napoleon's enemies are working to undermine him, and Filipe knows better than anyone that things are going from bad to worse.

Supply shipments are coming less and less frequently — and what does come is of poor quality. Faced with this serious problem, he and his men do as they have always done, they improvise, and make good use of the food the gatherers and hunters bring.

The spectre of hunger is not the only ghost that haunts the camps. Diseases, known and unknown, are rampant; to his great sadness his friend and great kitchen partner, Guion, who had been ill for some time, is dead by summer, the very season when life is supposed to blossom.

*

* *

Meanwhile, Napoleon has set his sights on Egypt, hoping to expand both the French Empire and his own status. The Directory, the all-powerful governing committee of the First French Republic, agrees to dispatch Napoleon to the region, under the guise of blocking Britain's access to India. Secretly, they see an opportunity to remove an overly ambitious general, whose popularity following his success in Italy, is potentially troublesome.

But history has a way of telling its own story.

Despite ultimately suffering defeat at the hands of the British, Napoleon's Egypt campaign enters the realm of legend, in part due his own talent for propaganda, but also because of the very important scientific work being done by the relatively large contingent of scientists and scholars who had accompanied Bonaparte for the purposes of studying Egyptian culture and civilization. Among their significant achievements is the discovery of the Rosetta Stone.

Ultimately, the British get the better of the French, sinking their ships in the harbour and effectively stranding Napoleon's army. With his own reputation in the balance,

Bonaparte sees a new chance for glory. France is again at war with the forces of Austria, Britain and Russia, while internally the country once again threatens to tear itself apart, with the governing authorities in Paris in a shambles. Napoleon seizes his opportunity and sneaks away to France, where he engineers what would become known as the coup d'état of 18 Brumaire, overthrowing a weak and fractured Directory, and installing himself as First Consul of France

Napoleon and his allies quickly move to consolidate his position, introducing a new constitution that gives him sweeping powers. A sham referendum is held in which the new constitution is ratified with 99% of the vote in favour. With all the powers of a dictator, Napoleon would remain a bellicose and authoritative figure until his abdication and exile to Elba in 1814.

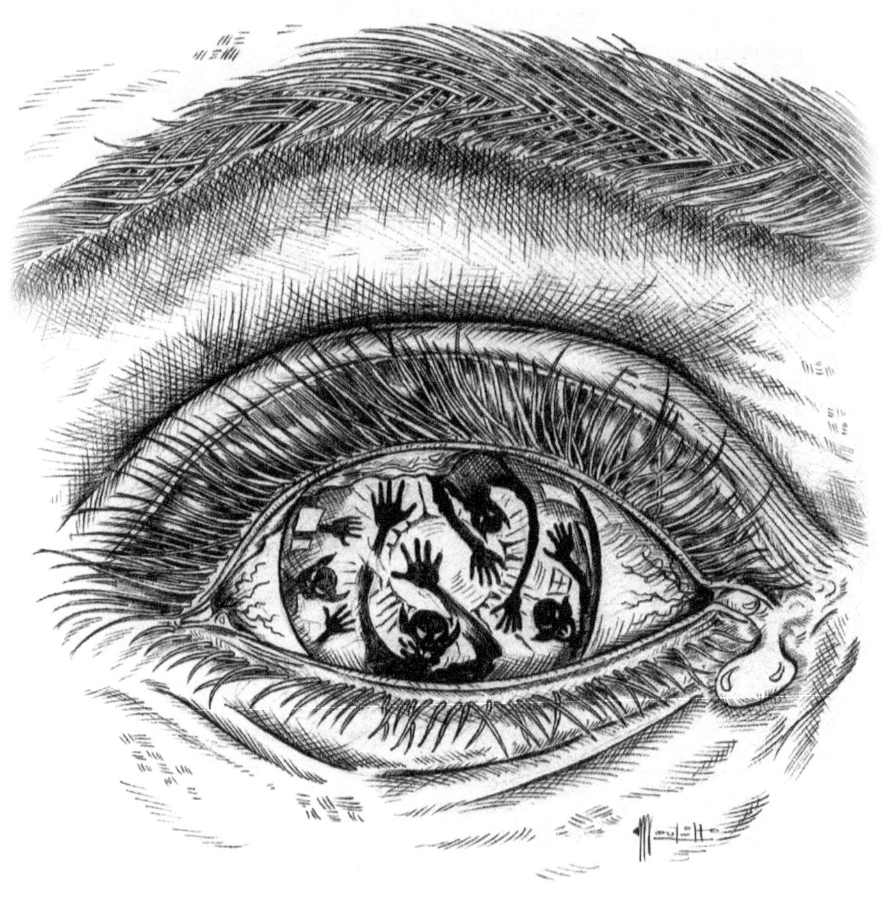

Tereza imagines she can hear the screams of lost souls.

CHAPTER 25

A grave undertaking

"Paris has another Paris under herself,
a Paris of sewers, which has its streets, its crossings,
its squares, its blind alleys, its arteries, and its circulation,
which is slime, minus the human form."
Victor Hugo

We shall now take a break from the endless misery of war and travel back in time a year or so, to that fateful day after the terrible incident at Francesc's house.

We find Tereza, still hiding in the secret closet behind the cheap wines, where Francesc kept his deeds and other important documents and treasures. She'd been there all night, listening to the sounds of the men rummaging and rifling through the house, terrified of being discovered.

At some point the men must have found something of interest – the petty-cash box in Francesc's office by the sounds of things. Luckily this appeared to have been enough for the miserable worms because they had left shortly thereafter, chuckling among themselves and congratulating each other on a fruitful night's takings.

Thankfully, the idiots had not had the brains between them to imagine that there might be a secret vault, where a man such as Francesc might hide his fortune, and where a kitchen maid might hide herself. This was their first error in judgment. It turns out that they had also made four other mistakes that night.

First, they had come away with very little for their effort, despite potentially earning the title of murderers. And even there, they had failed. Reasons two, three and four were the other three residents of the house whom they had also failed to kill.

Now, as Tereza finds the courage to emerge from the hidden room, she hears another man entering via the kitchen door. He's talking to someone – Filipe? Mon Dieu, is he alive? She hangs back just long enough to hear the man heft Filipe over his shoulder and leave. She would later learn that this man made his living delivering drunks, street urchins and other debilitated souls to the various recruitment centres that had become part of life during these perilous times.

But this information is of no consequence to her now as she creeps from her hiding place to discover a lifeless Francesc, sprawled on the kitchen floor. Coming closer she discovers that he is still breathing, but only just. She's unsure what to do, but decides to risk leaving him on the floor, and to the mercy of the fates, while she rushes out to fetch Michel, the local physician.

While Michel ministers to Francesc, Tereza tries to think of a plan to rescue her boss and hide him from sight, lest the same three ruffians return to finish the job.

Coincidently, it's the city itself that provides the answer.

*

* *

Paris, at that time, had a very Parisian problem. As the world approached the end of the 18th century, the city's popularity among the living had made it one of, if not the, largest city in Europe. But this eminent distinction also meant that it had a population problem of an entirely different sort — its graveyards simply could not contain the correspondingly large and growing contingent of the dead. Cemeteries were full to bursting. And as if the effluvia from the methane being released by the rotting bodies were not enough, there are many stories of the gas spontaneously combusting on occasion. The City of Lights became the city of exploding dead bodies.

Ironically, despite the foul stench, or perhaps because of it, Paris developed into one of the world's perfume centres, undoubtedly due to the ingenuity of its perfume alchemists.

Matters became particularly unbearable around 1780, when, following a period of sustained rain, some of the larger cemeteries, like the famous Holy Innocents' Cemetery, literally overflowed, and released their decomposed bodies, zombie-like, into the streets. The city authorities had no choice but to order the closure of the many of the cemeteries and forbid any further burials from taking place until a solution could be found.

The answer lay in the City's own unique topography. Paris was the site of innumerable quarries and mines that had over the years been dug to exploit the rich prehistoric mineral deposits, formed over hundreds of millions of years, and that been a significant source of wealth and development for the city and surrounding regions.

The literally hundreds of kilometres of underground tunnels left over from as many years of mining activities would make the perfect alternative resting place for the bodies. The macabre, but necessary, work of transferring the remains to their new underground resting place was begun in earnest. An entrance to the mines was built just outside the city gates, which later appropriately came to be known as the "Gate to Hell".

It is said that as many as six million individuals came to be buried here, including the likes of Georges Danton and Maximilien de Robespierre, who met their own Waterloos during the French Revolution; as well as other important characters from French history, such as Charles Perrault, who gave us some of the world's best loved fairy tales, in the form of Little Red Riding Hood, Cinderella, Puss in Boots and Sleeping Beauty.

*
* *

As luck would have it, there is a man who calls at the restaurant every morning to collect any unsold bread, which he takes and distributes to the construction workers working in the very same old mining tunnels and quarries that we have just learnt about.

This particular morning is no exception, and when Julian Petit (no relation), knocks at the door, Tereza wastes no time on the usual pleasantries. "Julian, thank God you're here. Forget about the bread, I need your help."

Together, they pile Francesc's broken frame onto Julian's cart, where they conceal him under a tablecloth and two dozen or so loaves, so that they can move him to one of the nearby tunnels via one of the less conspicuous airshafts. There they commandeer some of the workers' equipment and improvise a makeshift recovery ward; a mattress, clean sheets, alcohol for dressing the wounds (and other medicinal purposes) and a couple of wooden basins. Michel, the physician, provides various other medicines and advice - this is no place for a wounded man. Tereza agrees that it's far from ideal, but it's better than waiting around for the would-be murderers to return.

If the brutes had bothered to return to the scene of the crime, they would have seen a sign hanging above the door that read "Under Renovation due to New Management." As it happened, they were not seen or heard of again, and are believed to have disappeared into the ranks of Napoleon's army, along with thousands of others indistinguishable from one-another.

For Tereza, a devout Catholic, life among the skeletons and human remains is as about as close to a living hell as she ever wanted to get. She imagines she can hear the screams of souls, disturbed form a peaceful rest, or worse, still trapped in limbo, condemned to wander the tunnels endlessly looking for a way out. But she steels herself, and as time goes by, begins to fear the imagined voices and indecipherable noises less. Francesc, too, has begun to heal.

One day Tereza is kneeling beside Francesc, offering her daily prayer, when he sits bolt upright in his makeshift bed and grabs her by the arm. "Jesus, Mary and Joseph! By the saints, do you want to give me a heart attack?" she shouts, "Never do that again. I thought the dead had come to life."

Francesc smiles painfully, "My dear Tereza, only you would have brought me to such a place. If not for your prayers, I might have thought I had gone to hell."

"I mean it," said Tereza.

They both laugh.

Francesc grimaces, "Don't make me laugh. My ribs hurt."

"We'll I'm just glad you're alive. Now, let's see what we can do to get you out of this place full of lost souls."

Tereza tells Francesc about Filipe's disappearance with the unknown man. They talk for a while, before she brings up the idea of what their next move should be, "Shall we go back to the restaurant?" she asks.

No, I have a better idea. I have to get a letter to Mme la Boar. We must denounce these scoundrels who nearly killed me and did God knows what to Filipe. And then we shall away to the house Filipe spoke of in the countryside, where we will regroup and make our plans.

The deaths of three scoundrels.

CHAPTER 26

Marengo

"One man's meat is another man's 'poisson'."
To paraphrase Lucretius

Filipe had lost contact with Napoleon after the coup, in part due to the endless political manoeuvring in Paris and the General's own predilection for showing up where he was not wanted. By Filipe's recollection, the last time the two had spoken must have been at Marengo. On that day he had gone to meet the young hunter-gatherers to look over their kill and decide what to cook the troops for supper. As he approached their small encampment, he had noticed three burly soldiers talking aggressively to the youths. He didn't have to hear the entire exchange to know that the soldiers were extorting money from the younger men.

The young chef had been horrified to recognise the faces of the extortionists. Ghosts from a past life he had hoped were well and truly exorcised. A shiver ran up his spine and raised the hairs at the nape his neck. Here were the very same good-for-nothing rogues who had broken into Francesc's restaurant, murdered the old chef, and left Filipe lying in a pool of his own blood, also dead, for all they knew. He took a deep breath and approached.

The men had given no indication that they recognised Filipe. Instead, they had glared at him coldly until they realised that he outranked them, and moreover was clearly not to be intimidated. They all turned, about to slink sullenly back into whatever rathole they'd come from, when the tall one, Lieutenant Trusseau, the very same one from the party, and later, the restaurant, spoke. "I'm sorry, Captain, but I have a certain impression that maybe... I say maybe before … haven't we seen each other somewhere?"

With an extreme effort to keep his wits about him Filipe had answered as casually as his beating heart would allow, "No, I believe not, Lieutenant. If we had, I'm sure I would have remembered."

"My apologies, Captain, war plays tricks on the mind."

As they sauntered away, Filipe had stared after them, appalled and relieved at the same time. A moment later he was startled by a hand on his shoulder. He recognised Napoleon's ordonnance regarding him sincerely, looking like he had something on his mind. "Captain, the General asks if you would cook for him personally tonight. He expects dinner at 8pm sharp, following a meeting with some of the local clergymen."

Nodding his head in agreement, Filipe had watched the ordonnance leave before turning his attention to the young hunter-gatherers once more. They had all been sitting at a small table that was clearly used as a gutting and de-boning station. By all accounts the lieutenant and his men had been extorting the auxiliary staff for some time – from very shortly after they'd all marched out of Paris, in fact. Protection money, they'd called it. Protection from what? Filipe had wondered. The only ones who were going to need protection now were the extortionists themselves.

He had clenched his fists, quietly thanked the young men for their time, and stalked off. Retribution would have to wait, unfortunately, since there was work to be done.

Filipe's mood had not been helped by the shambolic scene that awaited him at the officers' kitchen that evening. The chicken that had arrived from Bresse earlier had been butchered so badly it was hardly worth talking about, eggs had been loosely thrown into a basket such that many were broken, and the kitchen itself looked as though it had been ransacked by a marauding horde of badgers. He would have to come up with something quickly. If this was going to be his chance to talk to Napoleon face to face about his plan to bring peace to the world, then his food had better live up to the promise.

A thought crossed his mind. He remembered that some of the hunter-gatherers had been collecting crawfish from a nearby river. He called to his kitchen assistant, Dominique, and instructed him to see about getting a batch for their purposes. They were in luck. Dominique returned with a goodly batch of still-wiggling river-crustaceans and a basket of ripe tomatoes.

One brief cleaning of the kitchen later, and Filipe was going over what was needed for Napoleon's dinner with his young assistant.

One badly butchered chicken, cleaned up and cut into acceptable pieces

Crawfish

Eggs

A good knob of butter

Chopped mushrooms

Finely chopped onion

Garlic (of course)

Bay leaves

Thyme

The fresh tomatoes

Parsley

Salt and pepper

Stock, freshly rendered from the carcasses of the very same chickens they started with

First, they seasoned the chicken pieces with salt and pepper, and placed them in a deep skillet over a relatively high heat with plenty of butter and a dollop of olive oil to stop the butter from burning. Once the chicken had begun to undergo the delicious Maillard caramelisation, they de-glazed the pan with wine, added the onion and bay leaves, sprinkled in the mushrooms and turned down the heat. When the whole lot was simmering away nicely, they added chopped tomatoes and topped up the skillet with the chicken stock.

Next the crawfish were lightly fried in butter and garlic and added them to the simmering goodness of the dish.

As a final touch, the dish would be served on a bed of rice, topped with a fried egg, and garnished with parsley. And salad on the side. Delicious.

Filipe and his assistant had gone into Napoleon's tent thinking he'd quickly shoo them away. The great man looked up from a document that he was reading and indicated that Filipe should join him at the table. "Today, you and I are going to have dinner together. It's been a long time since we talked! So, tell me, have you gotten yourself a name yet nameless cook? I am tired of my officers' company, and I thought I'd entertain myself with your presence."

Filipe was a little surprised, but not overly so, after all, this had happened before.

He opened a bottle of the General's wine, a Chambetin-Clos-de-Bèze, a heady little Pinot from Burgundy, which also happened to be a favourite of Filipe's. He served Napoleon and sat down quietly, waiting for the General to direct the proceedings.

Napoleon ate surprisingly calmly. He was known for eating fast, but tonight he took his time to savour the food, as though the moonlight had soothed his animal soul somehow.

"I was sorry to hear that your friend passed away, the chef, what was his name, Touchot? He did a lot for the troops. I sent an emissary with some gold talents for his wife and daughters. He was a good man."

Filipe was more surprised to learn that his friend Guion had a family than he was at Napoleon's apparent generosity.

The General had been in no mood to dwell on the subject of death and changed the subject before Filipe could answer, "So what name shall we give you then?"

If ever there was a time to speak, thought Filipe, now would be it. But the truth could be a complicated thing. "I fear that I have been less than completely candid. But what I did, I did for my own survival."

Napoleon looked up from his plate, "Oh?"

"There was a time when I really could not remember my name; that part is true. In fact, I joined the army not remembering anything about my life before. But over time I gradually started to remember more, until it all came back to me."

Napoleon put down his fork and wiped his mouth on a pristine white napkin.

"My name is Felipe Pierre Lacroix, son of Jean Pierre Lacroix."

"A good French name," said the General, causing Filipe to flinch, "well… why did you not give your name to the scriveners once you knew it?"

"If you'll allow me," said Filipe, I need to tell you the full story, and then perhaps you will forgive me for not divulging the truth earlier."

Filipe had begun to tell his story. Of his early life in Italy. Of his mother and grandfather. Of his father's life as a pirate. And all the events that led up to the party at Chateau Blosseau.

Napoleon had listened intently. At the point in the story where the great party came up, he could hold his tongue no longer. "Ah! la Boar's party. I knew it. You. You were one the cooks at the great party in my honour. What a night. The food. The wine. The tremendous spectacle of it all."

The great General had been as animated as Filipe had ever seen him. "I'm sorry to interrupt you, but your story is more interesting than I had imagined. And by the way, so is this food. You must tell me what the secret is. When I am back in Paris, I will have Marie Antoinette's chef do the same. But I fear my enthusiasm gets the better of me, please continue."

Filipe had continued, elucidating the events that led up to the massacre at Francesc's restaurant, and his subsequent loss of memory and involuntary enlistment in the French army.

"A magnificent story, Captain. But why did you not tell us your name the moment you found out? Do you know what makes a great leader? It's knowing how to read the eyes and soul of his soldiers. And I always thought you had a deeper story to tell."

He savoured a swig of the wine. "We are kindred spirits, you and me. From the day we met, I knew we had more in common than just a uniform. I ask again, what possessed you to keep your name a secret?"

"Three reasons:

"The first was that I felt I was in danger and didn't know who to trust. The only thing I could remember was that I had been attacked. By whom or for what reason I did not know. So, when the man who took me to the recruiting station dropped me off, I saw it as an opportunity to hide until I was able to figure out what to do next. Until I could discover who had attacked us."

"And did you find them?"

"By chance I did. They are here among us now. Part of your army. I caught them this very day, freely walking among the troops, extorting money from the auxiliary staff."

Napoleon's look blackened. He looked toward his waiting guard, and then back to Filipe. "We shall see about that," he said, before seeming to file the thought in his mind for reference with a wave of his hand.

"And the second point?"

"The second point, as you may have already discerned, is that I am half Italian…" here Filipe had paused to gauge the reaction. None came, so he had continued, "Well, we were about to march on Piedmont. I was afraid that I would be persecuted by my own brothers before we even reached the border."

"I understand that too," said Napoleon. He looked like he was about to add something more, and then caught himself.

"And the third?" he said after a careful pause.

"The third is a belief, a philosophy, that I carry in my heart, and that I have wished to discuss with you, even since I saw you at the party in Chateau Blosseau. If it please the General, I can elaborate…"

Before Filipe had been able to continue, an officer had barged in with a snappy salute, interrupting him mid-sentence.

"What is it man? Can you not see we're in the middle of something?"

"I beg your pardon sir. Your orders were to alert you immediately of any change in our enemy's status.

"Well? Spit it out man. My appetite wanes with your bumbling."

"Sir, as predicted, the Austrian Army is on the move. We must hasten if we are to cut them off."

The dinner had been over before it had really begun, and so had Filipe's chance to tell Napoleon of his great idea. Before he knew it, the General was buckling his swords and making for the door of the tent. At the last moment he turned and addressed Filipe, "Well, Major, it seems our discussion will have to be continued at a future date. I promise we shall have our time together – I am now more than just a little curious about your third reason. In the meantime, give the clerks your name so that we may formalise your existence, eh." And with a smile he was gone.

History would not remember Filipe's name. Marengo Chicken would be credited to another chef. And as for the three rogues, well…let's just say they hadn't bothered anyone after that day. They were found hanging from newly erected gallows.

Filipe hadn't wanted their deaths. He had wanted a world without violence and unnecessary death. But the deed was done, and Napoleon had sent his message loud and clear. Among the rank and file, the execution was considered fitting, and had simply reinforced the General's legend.

Filipe reads aloud from the book.

CHAPTER 27

Leda and the Swan

"Was this the face that launched a thousand
ships and burnt the topless towers of Ilium?"
Christopher Marlowe, Dr Faustus

With Napoleon perpetually off on some belligerent errand, Filipe had returned to Paris, wanting to know what had become of Tereza. The city was not the same place he had left behind on that fateful day some years earlier. He made his way to the old neighbourhood, hoping to see a sign or a face he recognised. Francesc's restaurant was no more; a sign painted in the window announced that it was now a fabric shop.

Forlorn, he had entered the shop to find the home he once knew unrecognisable. A striking, twenty-something dark-skinned woman appeared from the back and greeted Filipe cheerfully, "Can I help you *cher?*"

Taken aback, Filipe answered somewhat tentatively, "I, uh, well, I was looking for the owner…the previous owner, Chef Petite and his assistant Tereza. I don't suppose you know what happened to them? Where they went?

The woman spoke in a French accented with a North African lilt, "I cannot say *cher*, but if you have time, you could wait for the mistress of the house, who I expect to come back closer to the evening."

Filipe was tired and hungry. He needed to be somewhere familiar. He mounted his horse and headed for the only other place he knew, Rebecca's inn. Thankfully, the inn was just as he had last seen it, complete with the little hand-painted blue and white sign.

*

* *

Filipe's horse is a magnificent Arabian whose coat is so black it shines an intense gunmetal blue in the sunlight. Filipe has named him Vesuvius as a homage to his grandfather's stories of old Italy. He had acquired the horse from an old Saracen who had allied himself with Napoleon during the Egypt campaign. On accompanying the French army back to France, the man had bartered the horse for an old rifle that Filipe had won from his old friend Guion Touchot in a game of piquet. The Saracen had declared the beast too temperamental and was happy to see the back of him. Under Filipe's light touch, the animal is as docile as a bird.

The young captain in his military regalia looks like a prince as he dismounts. He's grown into a tall, handsome young man with sandy brown hair and striking blue eyes. His broad back and muscular arms are particularly noticeable to a nearby group of young ladies, as he removes the saddle and saddlebags.

Whether he notices their exaggerated sighing and giggling or not, he gives no indication of it. When it comes to women, he is still very much boy, naïve to their flirting, and seemingly immune to their wiles.

The reception area of the little inn is empty and quiet. There is a small bell attached to the ceiling with a thin chain. A sign reads Ring bell for attention. He is just about to do just that when his eyes fall on a book, open on a coloured illustration of a naked woman and a swan.

He reaches for the book and turns it toward himself so he can see the contents better. In the illustration, the naked woman is painted in close embrace with a swan. Below the image is the inscription, A reproduction of Leda and the Swan, by Cesare da Sesto.

He turns the page and begins to read aloud, as he has done many times in camp from Napoleon's many books to an audience of foraging children and kitchen urchins.

Leda, daughter of Thestius and wife to the legendary King Tyndareus, was among the most beautiful of all the Spartan daughters. Some quietly spoke of her beauty rivalling even that of Queen Sparta herself.

This is a story Filipe knows well, he continues in his best story-telling voice.

According to legend, Zeus, jealous that he could not possess Leda as his own, transformed himself into a swan and ravished her. Later, Leda also lay with her husband. From their collective commingling came four offspring, half mortal, half divine – Helen and Clytemnestra, and Castor and Pollux.

The girl, Helen, inherited her mother's beauty and grew into a woman of striking exquisiteness. Just like her mother, she inspired a great jealousy in men, who desired what they could not have. Theseus, overcome by his own folly, kidnapped her, and raped her before setting off on another foolhardy and ill-fated mission into the Underworld. With Theseus occupied with his own struggles against Hades, Castor and Pollux rescued Helen, and return her to Sparta.

Stories of her kidnapping by the mighty Theseus served only to heighten the legend of Helen's beauty, and many suitors vied for her attentions; warriors, kings and princes, powerful men bearing gifts and promises. Her father, not wishing to make enemies of these formidable men, devised a cunning stratagem – to let the Fates decide. A simple competition by drawing straws would determine who would marry Helen. But before the decision was made, Tyndareus made the suitors swear a solemn oath, that no matter the outcome, they must all agree to defend the chosen husband, with military assistance if necessary, in any dispute that might arise henceforth.

Menelaus emerged as the winner. He married Helen and became ruler of Sparta alongside Helen after Tyndareus and Leda abdicated their thrones.

Now, many stories would end at such a happy juncture. But ancient Greece was not a place of ordinary men or ordinary stories.

In another part of the country, a young man named Paris had gained the attention of the gods due to his charm, intelligence, honesty, and moral judgment.

The gods called upon Paris to arbitrate in a divine contest to decide who was the most beautiful among the three goddesses, Hera, Athena or Aphrodite. Aphrodite tricked Paris into choosing her by offering the love of the most beautiful woman in all of the world, Helen of Sparta. Paris led a raid to steal Helen away from Menelaus, but she fell in love with him and the two eloped and fled to Troy.

Tyndareus invoked the oath that had been made among Helen's erstwhile suitors. The powerful men of Greece launched against Troy.

The face that launched a thousand ships, Filipe thinks to himself.

Just then a girl appears from behind the curtain just beyond the reception. She must be about sixteen, but already Filipe could see that she is on the cusp of becoming a striking young woman.

As Filipe looks up, she says, "I heard you reading. Don't be shy on my account, please…go on…you read very well."

"I'm sorry mademoiselle, I didn't mean to intrude. I entered and there was none here but this book."

The girl smiles mischievously at Filipe and teases, "How do you know I am a mademoiselle and not a madame?"

Filipe blushes, flustered, said, "…but surely…"

"I'm teasing you Filipe." She emphasises his name for effect.

Discombobulation turns to surprise on Filipe's face at the sound of his name.

"You don't recognise me do? I'm Ana, Rebecca's daughter. You were here with your father. I think you must have been ten or eleven only. But I remember you well.

And with a huge smile, she extends her hand to him giggling, "And yes, I am a mademoiselle."

"You look like Helen of Troy," he blurts. He's now utterly embarrassed by his own awkwardness, "Gosh, a thousand pardons…what am I saying…yes little Ana…of course I remember." The resemblance to her mother was now painfully obvious.

Ana starts to laugh. But her humour is cut short by the arrival of a lieutenant in the French Army. The man, perhaps not expecting to see Filipe in his full regalia, drops his hat, and then while reaching to retrieve it, bumps his head on a chair.

Filipe looks on with a mixture of amusement and exasperation at the man, who now has found his bearing and salutes sharply. "Major, my apologies, you are a hard man to find. Britain has broken the peace with France, and your country needs you back at the front. By order of the General, you are required to report to the Sixth Regiment without delay. We are here to escort you."

He turns to Ana, who has a curious look on her face, as though she were thinking deeply about something. "Do you remember, Filipe, when I was a little girl, I said that I was going to marry you?"

Now it's Filipe's turn to wear a curious look. A flash of memory serves up the image of a precocious little girl with a slightly dirty face, standing very close to where she stands now, her face a bright in contrast to the dark mood that informed their last meeting. He remembers well her words; at the time they seemed more funny than serious.

"I remember. But I thought you could not be serious."

"Will you return to me? When you have done your duty? I'll be waiting, Major Filipe, of the Sixth Regiment."

With that she turns and darts away, just as she had done all those years ago.

Filipe feels a small pull at his heartstrings, but quickly dismisses the feeling and reclaims his bearings. "Now lieutenant, if you would lead the way."

Ana sits in the parlour of the inn, contemplating this brief encounter with Filipe. His arrival had been a very pleasant surprise. His swift departure had taken some of the wind out of her sails. She hadn't even had time to deliver the letter to Filipe. She turns the folded paper over in her hands. It's from Francesc; he and Tereza are alive and waiting for him at his property outside of Paris.

As surely as there is room for dessert, there is room for peace.

CHAPTER 28

The conversation

"History is written by the winners."
Napoleon Bonaparte

With the warmonger of Europe becoming more and more powerful and unpredictable than ever before, Filipe finds himself being flung across the continent seemingly without rhyme or reason. The endless field operations mean that he has no time to travel back to Paris. And when he does finally get time off, the distance is simply too great to cover and be back in time for the next campaign. He finds himself dreaming of Ana while the world around him becomes more nightmarish on an almost daily basis. The axiom "absence makes the heart grow fonder," has never been truer than it is now for Filipe.

One day, upon returning to his tent, Filipe finds a young corporal waiting for him with a small wooden box. "Sir, begging your pardon, but you are a hard man to find. I have travelled the length and breadth of Europe to deliver this into your hands."

Filipe places the box on his small field table and opens it. To his surprise and delight the box is full of letters from Ana.

You did well corporal, you have my thanks. This is indeed the most important delivery we have had in some time.

The corporal salutes snappily and turns on his heels.

Filipe tips the box out and rifles through the small pile. Some of the letters are dated years back. It's a wonder they've not gotten lost long ago.

He opens one and glances over the content. Ana's mother, Rebecca had passed away some time ago. This is sad news indeed and just adds to his feelings of discontentment over not having been able to return to Paris in the years since he last saw Ana.

The letters are all signed the same way; Come back to me, my love. I'll always wait for you. Your Ana.

He sits at his little table and ponders his place in the universe. The idea of running away back to Paris briefly flits across his mind. He wouldn't just be deserting his post, he would also be leaving the men, women and children of the kitchen who had come to depend on him. Also, the penalty for such an act was death. And that would be awkward. He'd seen traitors bayonetted to save bullets. It wasn't pretty.

No, there's no choice for him other than to continue as he has been doing. And hope to get an audience with Napoleon soon.

*

* *

By late into the first decade of the 19th century, Napoleon's Grande Armée had marched all over Europe, stamping the French Empire's mark onto the European consciousness.

The tentacles of France's influence now reach into the kingdoms of Italy, Spain, Belgium, the Grand Duchy of Warsaw (part of Poland), parts of Germany (Confederation of the Rhine), the Austro-Hungarian Empire, Prussia, Denmark and Norway.

It's an empire swollen beyond control. Where once the impulse was to fight for more territory, now the forces under Napoleon's command are simply fighting to maintain what they've conquered. The victories, such as they are, have been coming at an increasingly bloody cost to both men and resources. Tens of thousands of battle-hardened troops have fallen, not to mention any number of seasoned generals and high-ranking field commanders who are irreplaceable.

Filipe voices his misgivings about the general sustainability of the situation – to nobody in particular, since there is no one who can influence the course of history one way or another. Some of the other officers mutter among themselves, what does a cook know about war? And perhaps they are right. As magnificent a cook as he is, he is still just a cook. But as a senior officer with the rank of Major, he's privy to myriad conversations, strategies and secrets that give him a more than superficial insight into the current and future affairs of the great military machine that he's part of. He may not have graduated from the *école militaire*, as many of the other officers had done, but ten years of war with the Grande Armée have been his school. This has given him an uncommon perceptiveness and judgement when it comes to reading the signs on the prevailing wind.

And what the wind is telling him now is that Bonaparte's appetite for conquest is simply bigger than his eyes. Even with his reputation as a tactical genius on the battlefield, the inexperience among the ranks of his own army, when measured against the increased confidence of his opponents, is making life difficult for a general bent on Europewide domination.

Filipe is beginning to think that perhaps Napoleon isn't invincible after all. And if he, a mere chef, is coming to this conclusion, then it was only logical that European leaders are doing the same.

All it would take to tip the proverbial applecart was a spark; and that spark comes in 1812, when Napoleon's spies suggest that the Russians, his former allies, are plotting against France.

*

* *

Filipe keeps up his own campaign of trying to reach Napoleon to discuss the third item on his agenda. One day, somewhere between Paris and Smolensk, one of Filipe's assistants brings news that Napoleon will be holding a strategic meeting with his most senior field officers, after which he will dine alone in his private tent.

This is the opportunity Filipe has been waiting for. It will be tricky, however. At a time in which food has taken on a greater value to Napoleon's men than their own weapons, Filipe has done very little cooking, finding himself instead in the role of a food treasurer, elbows deep in paperwork rather than purée.

He has no choice but to bribe the chef assigned to the dinner to take an impromptu leave of absence, leaving Filipe himself to step into the breach. It costs him a good part of his savings, but in the end, he thinks, it's a necessary expense. And an investment in himself.

As for the menu, Filipe has some ideas about an alternative to the usual heavy fare coming out of the field kitchen.

He has observed that Napoleon leans over to one side in his saddle as he rides, as though something were bothering him – definitely not the posture of a man as skilled in the art of riding as the emperor who has conquered Europe on horseback. Something is awry, and to get to the bottom of it, as it were, Filipe approaches Bonaparte's physician. The man tells Felipe the truth under the condition that the conversation never leaves the canvas walls of the medical tent.

"Well, Major, the fact of it is that Napoleon suffers from the same ailments the Sun King, Louis XIV suffered from a hundred years ago. The emperor has an anal fistula. I had hoped it was nothing more than haemorrhoids, but I fear it is more serious."

He stops for a moment and observes Filipe for any signs of discomfort with the subject matter, before continuing in a slightly less serious tone.

"While our soldiers fight hand to hand on the battlefield, our emperor fights a rather more personal battle with his saddle, if you get my meaning."

The doctor has a sense of humour, thinks Filipe to himself, and amuses himself with the thought of King Louis engaged in an ongoing battle with the Netherlands, both geographical and somewhat more personal.

"I understand, doctor. I have been doing my own research into how diet might play a part in alleviating the discomfort and have discovered several approaches in the old Oriental cookbooks.

*

* *

The young chef sets about planning the meal, which will be rich in fibre – legumes, grains and lots of vegetables – to help the imperial bowel along. He knows that Napoleon favours thick broths, so black bean soup is an obvious choice. Next, he slices up oranges to serve as a palate cleanser between courses, but also for their vitamin C, which is believed to help reduce the inflammation and speed up healing.

He sautées vegetables lightly, replacing butter with olive oil. Dark green leafy spinach, broccoli and turnip greens to add a bit of zing. Also high in fibre and vitamins A and K and thought to be good for the blood.

And for dessert, sweet oats with raisins and honey. The cereal will absorb fat and help with the functioning of the intestine, while raisins are high in flavonoids, which are thought to have antioxidant and anti-inflammatory qualities.

Filipe muses that these are some of the simplest dishes he's cooked in years, and at the same time, some of the most important. He waits in Napoleon's tent for about fifteen minutes before the emperor is able conclude his meeting. Upon seeing Filipe, the big man cracks a smile and comes around the table to greet him, "Major! Filipe. Let me call you by the name that was so hard-won. What a pleasant surprise. How are matters in the quartermaster's store? I know there is no-one more qualified than you to take care of us. And how are you enjoying your new rank?"

"Thank you, sir. I appreciate what you have done for me.

"So, have you missed cooking, is that it? This is why you have decided to give me the pleasure of your company?"

"Yes, sir, in a manner of speaking. In fact, I have concocted a meal for the improvement of your health. But fear not, I have not forgotten your tastebuds."

Napoleon smiles an inscrutable, Mona Lisa smile, "Well now, from what I can remember, I am not ill."

"No, indeed sir, but if I may be so bold…"

"No, indeed," Napoleon interrupted, repeating Filipe's words for effect, "it is indeed that very quality in you, Major, your being bold, that I value above all else. You honour me by being sincere and direct, unlike those other political fools who surround me with their toadying lies. Please, carry on. Speak from the heart. It will make a welcome difference."

"Well, sir, at the risk of being indelicate, I have noticed that you suffer from a discomfort in the delicate areas. I would like to suggest that a change in diet might go some way to alleviating the situation.

"Ah. It seems intelligent men have greater powers of intuition and observation than most. I have been going through difficult times. My physician informs me that the stress of war can make a man ill in all manner of ways. Now, about dinner, you may serve it now, if you please. And join me. I could do with the company of an honest man."

At Filipe's command an aide appears and serves them both. Napoleon calls for bottle of wine to be brought, but on seeing the disapproving look on the younger man's face, declares, "Major, this is one time when your honesty is not desirable. Are you and my doctor in cahoots with each other to see who can make my life the more miserable? If not wine, then what shall a civilised man drink to quench his thirst?"

"I recommend blackberry juice, which even resembles wine in its colour."

Napoleon laughs, the idea of forgoing alcohol with his meal seems positively anti-French. "Bon, but know this, I will stop being a compliant patient the minute you and that infernal physician are out of sight.

"Now, what is this black broth you have made? It recommends itself well to the palate."

"I'm pleased you like it. It's a black bean concoction of my own creation, using beans native to South America. Nobody gives it much mind in Europe, but as a source of healthy protein, I recommend it highly."

"Well, it's delicious, reminds me of a cassoulet, I like it. Now, from your fidgeting, I suspect you're impatient to say something to me. Speak up Major, as is your wont."

"Well, sir, I believe you will recall a conversation we had some time in the past, in Spinetta Marengo, I think it was; we spoke of the three rogues plaguing the camps and I told you of my real heritage."

"Yes, I remember it well. The same conversation in which we discovered you had a name, given to you by a French father thankfully, even though you were born in Italy.

I'll let you in on a secret – my father was Corsican, which means I was also born an Italian, although later Corsica became part of France, so I became a Frenchman. As a child I suffered many an indignity at school because my accent was different from the other boys, so much so, that I affected a new way of speaking that became habit after a time. I recognised it in you the first time we spoke. You can take the man out of Italy, but perhaps you cannot take Italy out of the man, eh? But that's not the whole of it, is it? There is another topic on your mind – you were about to tell me something of great import when we were interrupted at our last meeting."

Filipe listens to Napoleon speak. The man's mind is as sharp and clear as any he's ever encountered. "Yes, sir, there is another consideration that I wished to unburden myself of."

"Now is as good a time as any…" says Napoleon.

"Well, it seems to me that we are at peace together here at the table … I mean we are eating peacefully, you on one side and I on the other, you are French, and I am Italian, we have different histories, and our lives have taken different courses. But here at the dinner table we have something important in common, this food…"

"I'm not sure that I quite discern your meaning…"

"Some of my fondest memories are of my mother cooking in our kitchen, sitting together with my grandfather and others, sharing a meal. It seems to me that the food always managed to create a high degree of peace and satisfaction between all those gathered. I have dedicated myself to trying to recreate this situation whenever I have had the opportunity to do so."

"Napoleon gives the faintest indication that he sees where this was going."

"You've said yourself that you remember the party at Chateau Blosseau, how many of the guests declared the food and the atmosphere to be outstanding. The party was such a success because of many things, but I venture to say the food was chief among them. It was a rallying point for something bigger. It allowed the guests to transcend their normal existences for a while and move to a different plane."

Napoleon's eyebrows perform their own military tattoo on his forehead.

"Bear with me for a minute, if you please, sir," says Filipe. "The thought came to me one day while I was reading a Hindu book on contemplations and meditations. The goal of meditation is to achieve a sense of inner peace – they call it Nirvana. I also noticed that the yogis placed their hands near their stomachs when in a meditative state. So, I began to think that perhaps food could also be linked to the achievement of some form of peace."

He looks directly at the emperor, "Are you not at peace now?"

Napoleon nods, not sure what else to do.

"Let me demonstrate my point," says Filipe, carefully trying to gauge Napoleon's appetite for metaphysics. I want to tell you about a dream that I had.

"In my dream you are walking across a bridge."

"A bridge? Where?" asks Napoleon impatiently.

"It doesn't matter. It could be anywhere. Anyway, you have the Grande Armeé at your back, stretching as far as the eye can see, four hundred thousand strong, the greatest army ever assembled."

Here Napoleon gives a satisfied nod.

"On the other side of the bridge is Wellington, with his British Army at his back. Equally fearsome, and equally ready."

Here Filipe pauses, again to gauge how close to the wind he might be sailing. "Well, in the middle of that bridge is a small table, such as you might find in any of Paris' bistros. My mentor, Francesc, and I, have cooked a meal for you to share. The two greatest generals in Europe, perhaps even in history, sit down and break bread together. At length, you begin to find common ground. As dessert arrives, the two of you have negotiated a peace treaty.

"This is my dream. This is what I have been so desperate to tell you all these years. This is why I have followed across Europe and beyond."

The emotion of the moment overwhelms Filipe, and a tear finds its way onto his cheek from somewhere. "Great nations and great leaders have their differences, but as surely as there is room for dessert, there is room for peace."

Napoleon laughs, genuinely amused by such a notion. "Forgive me, Major, you paint a pretty picture, very poetic indeed, even the reference to the mystical east, well researched if I may say. But you are naïve to think such a thing possible in this modern world. The human condition is not this way. Man is not built for peace. When we're not killing God's beasts, we're killing each other.

"Let me try to explain…

"When I was at the *Ecole Militaire*, I came across a book on biology. Are you familiar with that term, Major?"

"No, sir, I don't believe I am."

"No matter, it is the science of studying all life and living organisms, big and small – their origin, structure, function, growth patterns, manner of reproduction, their evolution, and importantly, their relationships to each other and the environment.

"Of course, this is a simplification, and the science itself is very complex. But there was one concept among the studies that I found especially intriguing.

"Do you know what all organisms in nature have in common?

Filipe feels that he's lost control of the conversation. "No sir."

"All organisms are governed above all by a singular desire to survive. The survival of their own species is paramount. All develop unique strategies to survive in their environment and compete against each other for resources.

"Take the animals in the jungle, for example. Every living thing from the smallest ant to the fiercest tiger is in a constant competition to stay alive. One might even say a war. A war to come out on top. The strongest devour the weakest, and so it goes, unending till the end of time."

Napoleon repeated the last line for effect. "Do you hear me, sir, I say the strongest devour the weakest."

The conversation is not going as Filipe had hoped it would.

"It is the same with mankind. For hundreds of thousands of years, it's been one rule only – survival of the fittest. We have not reached the top of the food chain by being weak. I certainly have not, I can tell you that, sir.

"And it's the same with the nations in this planet-sized jungle of ours; we must conquer or be conquered. There is no third way. Whether I want peace or not is irrelevant. France is surrounded by nations who would topple us from or place at the head of Europe."

Filipe doesn't quite know how to respond. When Napoleon says it, puts it in such scientific terms, the theory sounds like it makes sense in some kind of diabolical way. He takes a deep breath, hoping to suck some courage out of the night air.

"You make a strong argument, General, there is no disputing this fact. But if I may be frank, I believe there is one point in error in your description."

"Indeed," the corner of Napoleon's lip curls into the faintest of predatory smiles, "and what is that, pray tell?"

"Well sir, I believe that we are not mere animals. Certainly, we may be evolved from those beings. But is it not this very evolution that makes us more – to put it into a phrase – human, or perhaps the word should be humane? We are rational beings, capable of transcending our basest instincts. With the ability to engage each other in dialogue. Instead of eating each other, we have the capacity to sit at a table and share a meal, where each side can appeal to the civilised aspects of the other's nature."

Napoleon's face takes on an inscrutable look. There are not many people in the world who would dare gainsay the emperor.

Filipe adopts a low tone, "I know what it is to kill a man. I killed the rogues who murdered my father, and I delivered those three ne'er-do-wells to you, knowing full well what their fate would be. Their deaths weigh on my conscience. And I have seen more death than I care to remember as I have travelled across Europe in your service. It seems the price of death is always more death."

Whatever had been going through Napoleon's mind a few moments prior had clearly flitted off to some dark place to sulk on its own, and the man takes a more conciliatory tone, "Yes, Major, you make some good points. But the wars will continue, and we will invade Russia. I imagine that it might be amusing to invite the emperor, Alexander, to dine with us. You would outdo yourself, I have no doubt. But your talent is not enough to stay the course of history.

Filipe lowers his head. He feels somewhat deflated. Well, at least he's been able to get some of it off his chest, even if it hasn't gone as he had hoped it would.

The two men continue their dinner in silence.

It's Filipe who breaks the spell, "I beg your pardon sir. With the utmost respect, may I ask you a direct question."

"Sounds serious," says Napoleon.

"It is serious. I must directly ask you not to invade Russia. I feel it would come at too great a cost to you, and by extension, to France. Your army will face terrain unlike any you have faced before, and an enemy who knows the territory, not to mention the weather."

Napoleon looks deep into Filipe's eyes, and for a moment Filipe thinks he might have gotten through to some long-forgotten part of the emperor's brain.

"No. We are not creatures of peace. It is a fundamental law of the jungle. And we cannot go against nature."

Filipe and his band of raiders are ambushed.

CHAPTER 29

True grit

"In strategy, your spirit is what counts."
Miyamoto Musashi, The book of five rings

On the battlefield and in the political arena, Napoleon had no equal. His tactics and conquests became the subject of military studies in Europe and North America. He schooled himself by studying the tactics of the great Roman generals and borrowing from military writers the likes of Jacques Antoine Hippolyte and others. And then he took what he gleaned and honed his craft in battle.

His enemies quickly learned that Napoleon's army moved like no other they have ever encountered. Rather than one great massed monolithic force, Napoleon created a series of self-contained divisions, each with its own marshal or field commander. No longer facing the static lines of men they were used to; the enemy were simply unable to keep up with the novel manoeuvres and decisive tactics of this superior and more professional force.

When asked who the greatest general was, Napoleon's great nemesis, Wellington is reputed to have answered "In this age, in past ages, in any age, Napoleon."

But even the strongest of lions grows weak. And as he pushed further east, a new coalition consisting of Britain, Prussia, Austria, and Russia was organising against him.

Napoleon was on the move again, and where Napoleon went, Filipe was compelled to follow.

*

* *

The lands to the east are as dark and imposing as the horse Filipe rides. Cyrillic letters have replaced the familiar Roman alphabet, like a sinister code that curses their way. Even the Arabic khatt of North Africa had not seemed so alien. At least in Africa the people had smiled. Here the faces are frozen into gargoyle-like grimaces of pain and discontent. There is same hollow look in their eyes as he had seen in Guion before the older chef had finally gone to the big kitchen in the sky. As for provisions, he sees nothing worth picking, scavenging, or collecting. He sends word to his superiors about the situation. Nothing comes back in return.

The air out of the north is like an icy portent of things to come. As twilight falls at the end of each difficult day, a tired and disheartened army is greeted by an endless chorus of tar-black crows that transmogrify into bats as darkness finally comes, hissing through the air and waiting to devour any soul foolhardy enough to wander beyond the glow of the fire.

The spectral winds that patrol the camp at night pierce the canvas of Filipe's tent like it is nothing more than cooking parchment. The candle that he uses to read by at night stands little chance against these otherworldly forces. At times he swears he hears voices on the wind, eerily warning him of some impending doom; esssssscaaaape they seem to say.

*

* *

On a characteristically miserable, grey day Filipe encounters a cavalry scout attached to his division on his way back to make his report. "What's the matter, lieutenant, you look like you've seen a ghost?"

"No sir, not a ghost, but truth be told, I am not sure what I saw. I found a man from my unit, about twenty miles beyond the cliffs. His horse was gone, and he was undoubtedly dead, but what had been done to him was not the kind of thing I have ever seen before. His body had been stripped and some strange writing carved into his chest. Where his eyes had been, two copper coins peered out. This was not a military death, but rather some kind of religious butchering."

"Perhaps he fell afoul of horse thieves."

"It's conceivable, sir, but what of the coins? And the writing?"

"A warning perhaps, or something else. In some cultures, it is believed that the coins are payment to ensure safe passage to the other side."

The cavalry scout shivers visibly. "This was not the only sign. The villages were deserted, houses and fields abandoned, as though some evil hand had touched the land."

Filipe feels a tremor of uneasiness. He speaks, as much to alleviate his own discomfort as for that of the scout, "Perhaps our army has scared them off." In the back of his mind there's a hint of something more fearsome than he wants to admit to – the Cossacks, the dreaded "bears of the north".

Unafraid of any man or anything, the Cossacks were physically much larger than the French soldiers, with huge beards under enormous furry hats, and were said to wear necklaces made from the ears and teeth of their enemies. Filipe has heard tell that they shoot arrows better than the Mongols, ride better than the Turks, and where they go, death surely follows.

*

* *

Napoleon stubbornly pushes his men forward, deeper and deeper into enemy territory, overrunning the cities of Vilna and Vitebsk with surprisingly little resistance, and all but razing Smolensk to the ground. Students of history will appreciate that this was the Russians' plan all along – to lure the French forces further and further away from their supply lines. Knowing that they stand no chance against Napoleon's Grande Armée, Tsar Alexander's armies retreat beyond their reach, burning everything in their wake, leaving nothing for the French soldiers.

The Russians continue to play cat and mouse with the great French military machine, knowing that winter is coming and that the battle arena will be decidedly different once the really cold weather arrives.

Their moment presents itself in early September near the village of Borodino, in a battle that would prove to be one of the bloodiest of Napoleon's Russian Campaign, as well as a decisive moment in the lead up to Napoleon's eventual retreat.

Both sides throw everything they have at the other, with losses on the first day of fighting climbing as high as an estimated 70 000 on both sides.

They say that ice has no smell, but Filipe will never forget the smell of the snow on the morning after the great battle. Smoke and gunpowder mixed with the rusty metallic smell of blood. Pure hell.

Amidst the carnage the Russians have seemingly vanished into thin air, ostensibly leaving the road to Moscow wide open. But as the French would later discover, this is yet another ploy.

When they finally do make it to Moscow, what's left of the French Army finds a city in flames. Rather than subjugate themselves, the Russians have sacrificed their ancient city, leaving behind only vast quantities of vodka and no provisions. As his troops drink themselves into oblivion, Napoleon waits for an offer of surrender that never comes, until eventually, faced with the prospect of a Russian winter without supplies, the great general is forced to order his drunk and starving army to abandon Moscow.

Their retreat is dogged by merciless bands of Cossacks, low morale and a bitter cold that causes men and horses to simply die standing up. Filipe orders his kitchen staff to make stews from the horse meat for fear that the troops might resort to cannibalism in their depleted and starving state.

By the time the French forces reach Lithuania, their numbers have been reduced to a tenth of their original size, with the bulk of the men dead, deserted, wounded, captured, or just forsaken along the way. The once 400 000 strong Grande Armée is now anything but grand.

For the second time in his career, Napoleon abandons his army to the charge of another field commander, and flees, this time to Vilnius in order to regroup, before returning to Paris where rumours of a coup swirl.

Filipe once again finds himself without a lodestar to guide him, lost and disoriented, along with approximately 40 000 starving and beaten French soldiers desperately trying to flee the frozen hell of Northern Europe. Fate is not on his side, and after an ill-conceived raid on a grain storage barn, Filipe and his band of raiders are ambushed in a hail of gunfire. Despite being badly injured, Filipe somehow manages to make his way back to the column with a wagonload of grain.

There, along with just three remaining survivors from the original raiding party he is hailed as a hero for saving their starving comrades in arms.

His recollection of the journey back to Paris is a blur of pain and delirium, in which he is troubled by the same nightmares that had plagued him since they had crossed

into Russia. A ghostly wind taunts him as he dips in and out
of consciousness.

*

* *

When Ana sees Filipe, she's conflicted with feelings of relief
and desperation. It's been several years since she had seen
him last – when she had found him reading aloud from the
book at the inn. Most of her letters to Filipe had gone
unanswered and she had feared him dead. And now here he
is – on her doorstep once again, not quite dead, but certainly
halfway there.

Once the pieces of bullet that had lodged themselves
near the heart have been removed, the infection subsides,
and the doctors pronounce Filipe to be on the mend.
Fresh bandages, fresh air, fresh water, and lots of rest are
the prescription.

Francesc and Tereza have returned to Paris to be with
him as he recuperates. But so far he's been too weak to even
be aware of their presence.

Their turn for a joyous reunion will come soon enough.

The day of the wedding.

CHAPTER 30

The wedding

"Kiss me, Kate, we shall be married o' Sunday"
William Shakespeare, The Taming of the Shrew

Bouncing along in their rickety cart on the way to Filipe's farm, Ana looks over at her future husband and smiles. Filipe's recovery has been nothing short of miraculous, but then, he always did have a strong constitution. She takes a small leather bag from somewhere among the many folds of her dress and hands it to Filipe.

"What's this?"

"Open it. It's for you. For our future."

The bag is full of gold coins. It's difficult to estimate their worth, but Filipe sees that it's a significant amount. He opens his mouth to say something, but she beats him to it.

"This is my dowry, my love. Even though my father died a long time ago when I was a small child, he nevertheless entrusted this money to my mother in the hopes that she would guide me in making good decisions when I was of age."

"Ana my love. You are as noble as you are perfect for me. The old traditions are so quaint. I would marry you with or without a dowry, I think we have established that already. Besides, I have my own savings from my time with Francesc and of course from the army. And we already have a house. This is a beautiful gesture, but unnecessary. You should keep the money for yourself."

Ana leans over to give him an affectionate kiss and almost ends up landing on top of him as the cart bounces over a log. "Then it shall be ours, together."

*

* *

The happy pair plan to adhere to the popular matrimonial traditions of the time as much as possible. Filipe has bought two gold rings and has even had two pendants made using two halves of the same single gold coin in accordance with local custom. Ana has made a dress out of light blue cloth, since white is out of vogue. Some of Ana's friends have promised to bring a clairvoyant witch to the wedding, to interpret and bless their future together.

There are, however, some customs that they're not going to be able to follow. For one thing, both sets of parents are dead, so the customary contracts, guarantees and promises between family patriarchs, of land, houses, money and even animals in some cases, will not be possible. But this kind of thing is wholly unnecessary between the two of them anyway and is barely mentioned. There are plenty of reasons to trust each other beyond a mere signed document. Their marriage will be based on the principles of real love and mutual respect. Both been through too much for it to be any other way. They will be equals, and if any advantage is to be had, it will favour their future children. There's a common saying in these parts – there is more love among peasants with children than among the nobility for whom the idea of marriage is a political necessity.

They talk about these and many other things as they trundle along.

By and by they see the old farm gate in the distance that Filipe's father and Piotr had built after their return from Italy. The farmhouse, too, has undergone many improvements and renovations over the years, making it look rather more like a small chateau than the humble stone dwelling it once was. The central structure has been augmented by smaller structures on either side, forming a small courtyard. Beyond this a wine shed now overlooks a modest vineyard. The stables have been completely overhauled, with place for several more horses added alongside the original structure.

As they approach, a figure comes bouncing out of the farmhouse on those fabulous buttocks that Filipe will never forget. Margot! He hasn't seen her since his early days with the Sixth. How long has it been? Too many years to count.

She marches ahead of a veritable phalanx of women, who all hurry to greet Ana and whisk here away to do girly things. Francesc appears, close on their heels, and greets Filipe with a warm hug. He looks slightly older now, and is a bit plumper, but the blue eyes are still as piecing as the day they had first glared at a dazed Filipe as he sat on the floor of Chez Petit covered in custard cream and icing sugar.

"Mon Dieu, I cannot believe my eyes. I always knew you would survive. Even as I lay in those infernal catacombs, halfway between the living and the dead, I knew…" he grabs Filipe up in a hug that lifts his feet off the ground, which reminds Piotr how Filipe's own father used to pick him up.

*

* *

Filipe has been beaming from ear-to-ear since he arrived back at his home. His mouth literally hurts from all the smiling, and his arms ache from all the embracing. Old friends and acquaintances have been arriving in a steady stream. Familiar faces, some of whom he hasn't seen since they were children, and who are now grown up.

The throng is already some twelve hundred strong by all estimations and growing.

It's impossible to accommodate them all, but the weather is good, there's plenty of open ground, and in any case, many people have arrived in carts and wagons, or brought tents and canvas bivouacs of their own. Everyone's expecting a party.

Most have brought gifts, exotic and otherwise, to honour the couple - horses, goats, pigs and even a couple of Egyptian greyhound puppies are among the offerings. Many men and women who had known Filipe during the wars have brought gold and silver coins and whatever else they could afford for the friend who had once saved them from starvation. Some have brought fruit tree seedlings or flower cuttings, while others have arrived with barrels with distilled potato drink or mead.

Those more comfortably off have brought porcelain and other finery from Paris. Madame la Boar, not to be outdone by anyone or anything, had arrived earlier with a wagon full of typically extravagant furniture made in the South of France.

But undoubtedly the most unusual gift, if that's what it could be called, comes from an Italian peasant whose life Filipe had saved during the Piedmont campaign. The then young captain had removed a bullet from the man's side using a filleting knife and brandy for both anaesthetic and disinfection, then nursed him through two days of fever and delirium.

The peasant had arrived with his scruffy little two-year old daughter in tow. "Major Filipe, you once saved my life, and now I must ask that you grant me another boon. My wife has recently passed, and I fear I have fallen on hard times. I find I am unable to take care of my four daughters properly. Fortunately, the three older girls are of an age that they can take care of themselves, but the youngest needs a mother and a stable home. I ask that you and your wife-to-be take the little one in as your own and give her what I cannot.

Upon seeing the dishevelled state of the little girl, Ana's heart all but melts. Filipe, too, is moved. Without giving it a second thought, they both agree. "You'd better not back out on the wedding now, Filipe," says Ana, as she whisks the little girl away to be bathed and fed, "our family has already begun to grow."

Filipe concludes his conversation with the father of the child. "I know this must have been a difficult decision. We will take good care of her; you have my word as a fellow Italian." With this, he gives the man a pouch of gold coins.

"I cannot possibly accept," says the man, "I am already physically and spiritually indebted to you."

"Then think of it as a gift for your other three daughters," responds Filipe.

As the man takes his leave, Filipe wonders how many other fathers in Italy, Russia, Poland and elsewhere couldn't afford to look after their little girls. How many families had been destroyed by the steamroller that was Napoleon Bonaparte.

*

* *

In the days leading up to the nuptials, the atmosphere is abuzz with wedding preparations.

Francesc has all but forbidden Filipe from helping with the food, "This is not the week for cooking, Filipe, there will be much time for that in the future. Take care of your guests, renew old acquaintances, make new ones. Seeing the numbers arriving, I estimate we'll be as many as fifteen hundred by the day of the wedding – like cooking for Napoleon's Grande Armée again," he laughs at his own joke.

"But fear not, I have a good plan, if you'll hear me out.

"We'll make the most enormous barbecue you've ever seen – so big that it shall require twenty men to tend to it, and perhaps the fire will even be seen from Paris. On it we will cook twelve whole oxen and fifty whole pigs on the spit and two hundred chickens, in pieces, all of which we will

290

season beforehand with coarse salt, rosemary paste, garlic paste, white mustard, white pepper and nutmeg.

We'll bake two thousand baguettes, in specially constructed mud ovens. We'll bring the lettuce and fresh vegetables from the entire neighbouring area to make enough salad for the entire party, which will be accompanied by gallons of vinaigrette dressing. I have ordered four hundred kilograms of cheese, just for the occasion, and one hundred barrels of Bordeaux wine from an old supplier of mine, as well as as much beer and cider as we can drink.

As for sweets, there will be cakes with nuts and sunflower seed, and a mountain of pastries, rivalling even the ones we used to make in Paris.

And finally, Maria and the girls will be in charge of concocting a huge sangria that will require a hundred waiters to serve it on the day.

There should be enough to last for several days, including the wedding feast.

*

* *

When the big day arrives, it does so in a flourish of French sunshine that reminds Filipe of the sun that shone on him and his father as the crossed the Alps back into France all those years ago. Filipe's humble homestead has been transformed into great, joyous gathering. The smell of the wood-fired barbeque pits and searing meat hangs in an air already thick with anticipation. Everywhere he looks, people are expectantly making preparations, setting up tables and chairs, rigging canopies to protect the food, and themselves, from the sun, and carrying large blocks of ice from the barn to the serving areas.

A raised dais with an altar has been constructed about three hundred meters beyond the main dining area. Mary and the women had spent the previous day decorating it with flowers and ribbons and bibbons on every side, and bells, and buttons, and loops, and lace, to borrow from a favourite literary source. The whole thing forms a kind of open-air church, with chairs and cut logs lined up in rows where the pews would have been in a real church.

Filipe is inspecting the construction when his old friend, Rubens, arrives, along with the same old priest from the old country, the very same one who had buried his grandfather and mother. Rubens looks noticeably older, while the priest looks exactly the same as he did all those years ago.

By mid-afternoon the dining area is filling up quickly. Laughter and merry shouts can be heard over the sound of the musicians who have cleverly reserved their place under one of the many make-shift tents, out of the way of the sun. Apparently one of them is related to the clairvoyant woman who earlier had predicted sun, along with, predictably, a happy future for the couple. The same woman had also said that she had never read so many futures in one sitting, and that this was literally the greatest event she's ever participated in.

At some point the musicians change their tune. Everyone looks round as the bride and groom make their way toward the altar. Ana is holding tight to Filipe's arm, which is shaking visibly, even from the vantage point of the bar where Margo is holding forth to a collection of young men who seem enthralled by her ample assets.

If these same young men had bothered to cast their eyes toward the wedding party, they would have seen the bride veritably floating along in a light blue taffeta dress of her own design. Its simple construction, sans the traditional wooden bustle, is reinforced only with an internal layer of tulle and the most delicate of bamboo strips, which accentuate her figure, giving her the perfect hour-glass silhouette. She's as worthy a bride as any princess, and wears a veil of tiny roses, perfectly in keeping with the sylvan scene that plays out around them.

As they reach the specially constructed dais, Filipe bounces forward a pace so that he can help Ana up the step onto the raised platform. The priest is already waiting for them, glass of wine in hand, as he ushers them forward. They stand together as the priest begins his wedding sermon.

When he gets to a favourite passage from Genesis his rhetoric climbs up a notch, "…and God created man in his own image, in the image of God he created him; male and female he created them. And God blessed them. And God said to them, 'be fruitful and multiply…,' here he chokes on his own enthusiasm and reaches for the glass of wine.

In the confusion of the moment, Filipe decides this is his cue to kiss his bride, prompting a priestly deviation from the script, "Steady on Filipe, I didn't mean to be fruitful and multiply at this very moment…"

The crowd lets out an appreciative roar approval at the priest's ad libbing. Filipe just blushes and says, "Sorry, Father, it's just that I am nervous." Anna giggles a little.

The priest finds his rhythm again with the help of another swig of wine. "…romance is fun, but true love transcends all; it is the desire to attend each other for life. Today is also a celebration for the rest of us, for it is a pleasure for us to see love bloom, and to participate in the union of two people so delightfully suited to one another. And to have a couple of glasses in the process."

He looks at Filipe to see if there are going to be any further impromptu additions to the ceremony and winks, "And now, I pronounce you man and wife. You may kiss the bride, if you have any desire to do so for a second time."

Again, an eddy of appreciative laugher rises from the crowd, carrying their collective joy aloft like an air balloon rising in a thermal on a hot day. A blushing groom leans over once again and gives the smiling bride a tender kiss.

Filipe places the ring on Ana's finger, and the half-coin pendant around her neck. She replies by doing the same, with a ring and the other half of the coin.

The ceremony is over, and just in time, too, since the priest's glass is empty.

The happy couple jumps down from the dais and disappears into the throng of a thousand slightly tipsy well-wishers.

*

* *

Later that evening, in another part of the farm, Francesc encounters Tereza sitting by herself, crying. He sits next to her and asks, "Why this sadness my dear? Is this not a joyous day? The boy who tumbled through our window all those years ago is today a man. Is this not cause for celebration?"

"Oh Francesc, of course. Filipe is like a brother to me, and Ana a new sister. I'm not crying for them."

"Then who are you crying for?"

"I'm crying because you never noticed how I adored you. My feelings were out in the open, right under your stubborn Gallic nose, for all those years, and you never once acknowledged me."

The chef is genuinely surprised. He's an older man and she's a young woman with plenty of prospects beyond a crusty old chef. He had never dreamed of abusing their friendship in such a way. He says, "well, I…I must confess, I have a tremendous amount of affection for you. Let's celebrate the story of our friends' happiness today, and perhaps the next chapter will be ours. With that, he leans in to give her a small, half embarrassed kiss. She grabs him and turns the moment into a prolonged and proper kiss. "That's' better," she says, smiling now at his surprised look.

The last supper.

CHAPTER 31

The last supper

"Do not fear God,
Do not worry about death;
What is good is easy to get, and
What is terrible is easy to endure."
Epicurean text

Almost a full ten years have passed since the day of the great party and wedding. Life on the farm has taken on a pleasant routine. Filipe and Ana's adopted daughter, Marie-Charlotte, has grown into a plump and carefree young girl, and the couple have been blessed with triplets, Annette, Adrianne and Antoinette. Francesc and Maria had gotten married and had a daughter of their own, whom they called Filipa.

It's a happy little clan.

But fate is a funny thing and has a way of finding the cracks in even the most integral of family units.

On a stormy, but otherwise nondescript night, a stranger appears at the gate. In the darkness the man looks like a spectre from beyond the grave, come to collect a soul. His black cloak, sodden from the rain, clings to his body like a wet ghost. His horse, too, is as black as night, a dark lumbering shape, blowing hot steam from its nostrils and breathing with a deep rasping sound as though it longed to return to the other side.

If it weren't for the long-brimmed hat that kept the water from engulfing the man's face completely, and allowed Filipe to make out the man's eyes, he might have passed for something less than human.

Filipe pulls the animal's reigns and leads beast and rider to a dry barn. A religious person might wonder at the wisdom of turning one's back on such an apparition, but Filipe believes he has seen the man's face before, and if there is anything to dread, it's the message he has undoubtedly come to deliver.

Once inside the barn Filipe helps the man dismount, before deftly removing the tack. The military seal on the saddle confirms Filipe's suspicions. The man has been sent by Napoleon, or someone very close to the old emperor.

The two men stand looking at each other. Soldiers, both. One representing the present, the other a dark past. Napoleon's man speaks first, "The Emperor demands to see you, Major. I am under orders to bring you to him. I have come a long way and am in no mood to negotiate. Refusing this invitation is not an option; you will be shot as a deserter if you do."

The man's message is not a huge surprise to Filipe, although he is taken aback at the directness of the language. He measures his words carefully, "Good sir, I don't feel like a deserter. The war has been over for years, and I am certainly not hiding. You yourself obviously knew exactly where I could be found. The only thing I might be guilty of is not returning a worn-out pair of boots."

"That's not quite how the French army sees it. And most definitely not how Napoleon sees it."

Filipe wants to say that Napoleon and Grand Armée are no more. The failed Russian campaign and Waterloo have seen to that. Besides, the emperor is now languishing in an island jail off the coast of Africa somewhere. But he knows that Napoleon is not without influence still to this day, despite his remoteness from Europe. Saying no at this juncture could jeopardise everything he has worked so hard to create.

Unaware that Ana has crept into the barn silently, Filipe now turns and sees her. The look on her face is hard to discern; concern, certainly, but something else, too. Being the intelligent woman she is, she has appraised and understood that the situation is far more complex than it appears. Filipe's responsibility toward his family is paramount, but paradoxically, that might mean that leaving them for a short time is the only way to protect them. Felipe's decisions here tonight must take all of this into account. His family's best interests come first. She gives him an almost imperceptible nod. It's enough to give Filipe all the information he needs.

"Bon," says Filipe curtly, "we will go and see him. One last mission. But then I'm out. Officially."

It's clear that the soldier is tired. This is frankly the best outcome he could possibly have hoped for. His face shows visible relief for a moment before he recovers his military demeanour and responds, "Good, then it's decided. I will need a day to rest, as will my horse. And I would appreciate a meal and a place to dry out."

Filipe nods, and gently asks Ana if she wouldn't mind bringing a bowl of soup and bread. Then he turns to the cavalryman, "You will be comfortable here. I will send a man to see to your horse and provide you with blankets."

"Thank you," comes the response, and then after a moment of hesitation, the man adds, "I feel I need to caution you, as one soldier to another, your conversation with Napoleon is bound to be listened in on, also you will be questioned by the British soldiers after the fact. Be careful what you say. The old lion is significantly weakened, but he is nonetheless still a lion, so be on your guard."

Filipe looks at the man with some small amount of curiosity and smiles. It's going to be an interesting encounter indeed.

The ride to the port of La Rochelle will take a week or so. Filipe's Arabian could undoubtedly do with the exercise, and he informs his man to ready the animal for the journey.

*

* *

At the port, they make preparations for the voyage to St. Helena. They will sail out across the choppy waters of the Bay of Biscay and then south, around the bulge of Africa and across the equator before turning south-southeast toward their destination somewhere in the south Atlantic.

Filipe's horse has lost none of its temper around boats and creates such a commotion that Filipe eventually decides to disembark the horse and leave him with the port corporal, Jean Bittencourt, who coincidently Filipe knows from his time in the army.

"You won't need him on the island anyway," says Bittencourt, "he'll be more of a hindrance than anything else." Filipe agrees and leaves the horse, with instructions to look after him and exercise him well.

Four weeks at sea is enough to tire anybody out. Filipe is nowhere near the sailor his father must have been, and he's glad to be on dry land again, even if it is night time on a rocky, cold, windswept, inhospitable island. The lack of breakwater, as well as the barren landscape, only reinforce the idea of this rock in the middle of the ocean as an appropriate place for a jail.

The landing party, consisting of Filipe, the soldier who had fetched him at the farm, two British guards and a scrawny, shifty-eyed man who Filipe had not seen before, but who mysteriously appeared as they made shore, is transported by wagon across the stony ground until they reach a series of small stone houses. The dwellings are covered in moss and look anything but accommodating. This is a far cry from the balmy conditions of Napoleon's previous exile on Elba, but then, that might be the point.

The guards jump from the wagon and indicate that Filipe should accompany them into one of the structures. A small ante room is lit by candles and whale oil lamps and warmed by a modest fire and decorated with harpoons and whale eyes.

The two British guards make sure Filipe feels their presence, while the scrawny man sits near the fire, trying to make up for an obvious lack of blubber to keep him warm. A fourth man enters from a room off the side and the men begin to talk idly to each other in English, clearly assuming Filipe can't understand them. He can understand, of course, in part having learned English by reading Napoleon's many books written in that language.

They switch to French and the new man introduces himself as Napoleon's doctor. The two English guards speak passable French while the scrawny man has an accent that Filipe can't quite place. He introduces himself only as a captain. A spy, thinks Filipe, as he tries to fathom what might be going through the man's mind. The spy, for his part, meets Filipe's gaze with a piercing look that says I know your secrets. I can read your mind and your soul.

Read whatever you want, think's Filipe, I have no secrets, I am an open book.

After an unblinking minute, the man speaks again. "Major, allowing you to speak directly to Bonaparte goes against all our better judgement. But unfortunately, by the terms of his incarceration under the British, and on a humanitarian basis, we are compelled to allow it.

"We must warn you that there are to be no coded messages between the two of you. Anything you speak about will be followed up on and investigated, so my advice is to steer clear of any discussion on France or French politics.

"Please understand, we are not simply doing this to be unreasonable, but rather to curtail any talk that might lead to further war. Europe is in a state of sensitive peace. And we wish to keep it that way."

If only they knew, thinks Filipe. Did I not preach peace to Napoleon over and over again? Did I not try to prevent the invasion of Russia? "Your suspicious minds have nothing to fear from me gentlemen. We are on the same side as far as that is concerned. Perhaps you forget that I was an unwilling soldier in Napoleon's insane wars. I have seen a good many men lose their lives unnecessarily. And those who didn't lose their lives have sacrificed untold years to their own internal, personal wars that plague all soldiers and survivors of war.

"War robs men not only of their possessions, but of their dignity and their souls. You presume to stand before me in uniform and lecture me. Pff. I will help you in whatever way I can. And I will help Napoleon in any way I can. Because if there is any way I can maintain whatever fragile peace exists here on this island and in the world, I will do it. But do not mistake my presence for absolute compliance. I am not here by choice, but rather, because you dragged me from my family. The sooner I can leave this godforsaken rock, the better."

They had not expected such a response. There is a moment of hesitation before the scrawny man speaks again. "Your point is well made, but so I think, is ours. You will be escorted to meet your one-time commander, but remember, you will be accountable for your words and your actions."

With that, they escort him out into the cold night and toward a slightly bigger, two-storey house, about one hundred meters away. One of the guards raps vigorously at the front door, which opens to reveal a rather dishevelled man who we recognise from the beginning of our story as Louis Marchand. "Pah, these vultures in red jackets should not be allowed near doors. They are so uncouth that they must break everything they come into contact with. What do you want?"

One of the British soldiers responds in a mixture of broken French and English, "Go and tell the big man *qu'il a un visiteur.*"

The dishevelled Marchand retorts, "So, the cook with no name has finally arrived. I confess I thought he was nothing more than another one of Napoleon's delusions. The legendary kitchen Major who is just like the big man himself, half French, half Italian, and one quarter madman. Well, I suppose you'd better come in, before the shouting starts again from upstairs."

Filipe is not impressed in the least with this dirty ordonnance. Napoleon would never have countenanced such behaviour from his staff when he had known him. As they ascend toward the upper floor Filipe wonders how a man used to the great staircases of the palaces of Europe can ever get used to this narrow, rickety excuse for stairway that looks like it belongs in a Turkish prison.

The door to Napoleon's room is open. A voice from within shouts, "Leave me alone you Philistines, I'm writing."

Filipe recognises the voice, but there seems to be less of the commanding timbre than there once was.

Marchand speaks in the tone of a man used to being shouted at, "General, he has arrived."

Silence.

And then footsteps.

The big man appears at the door frame, book in one hand. He's older than Filipe remembers, not surprisingly, and somewhat fatter, his greying jowls unshaven. The eyes, however, have not changed. They retain that same fierce spark that Filipe once loved and feared in equal measure.

A look of recognition that might also contain a hint of affection flickers in those eyes. Napoleon puts a hand on Filipe's shoulder, "Ah, Filipe, the cook who once had no name. I hope you have been treated well; I find the British to be without refinement. Come in immediately, we need to talk." He swipes a pile of books from the small table and drags a chair nearer for Filipe to sit on.

He addresses Louis, "Bring more wood for the fire, and we'll have wine and cheese. And, Louis, you can tell those infernal Redcoats that they can stop skulking about, they'll get no secrets from me."

Then he turns his attention back to Filipe, "Sit, sit my boy, how long has it been? As you can see, they keep me in dire circumstances, but I play tricks on them. Who's to say who is winning. How have you been anyway? I learned from some of those loyal to me that you saved what was left of your regiment before you yourself were shot. Terrible business that."

Filipe is doing his best to keep up with the verbal stream of conscience coming for his old commander. He's long forgotten what seem to be curiously fresh memories for Napoleon.

The gush of words continues, "We did not accuse you of deserting the army because we understood the serious nature of your circumstances. Your life was at risk, and we allowed you to be removed back to Paris to heal. But we lost track of your whereabouts. I confess, I thought you may have succumbed to your injuries, although I hoped that would not be the case.

Well, you were sorely missed at Waterloo. Perhaps if I had had you to counsel me as you tried to do on previous occasions, the outcome might have been different."

Filipe can't believe what he's hearing. Did he just travel thousands of miles across the ocean to hear this man ramble on nonsensically?

Napoleon takes a sip of wine and continues, "There was a time when we talked and I confess I almost had you killed, but I was drunk on my ambitions and my ears were more useless than my eyes.

"I have brought you here because I don't know how long I have to live. I suspect the British are poisoning me, although they deny it. Nevertheless, I am losing my strength little by little…" The man grows silent.

Filipe thinks how small the once mighty man suddenly looks huddled in the armchair. He speaks, "General, I have come here at great pains to myself and my family, but I believe not to do so would have put us in greater discomfort, even danger. So, I must speak plainly, as you know I am wont to do. It's been more than a decade since our last encounter, and I had hoped to forget the years of wasted life that I was forced to sacrifice as I followed you on your campaigns. And for what? There is no glory here. Stuck on a cold, wet island, attended to by a dishevelled ordonnance and surrounded by soldiers loyal to another country. I advocated for peace, as I am sure you will recall. You had no need of my counsel then, why now, all of a sudden?

"Your Grande Armée bulldozed its way across Europe, leaving hundreds of thousands without dignity or hope. I saw the empty eyes, the suffering of women and children. I smelled death on the wind, as you brought hell to the earth. So, I ask you again, what possible benefit can you hope to gain from bringing me here?"

"You speak from the heart. I expected nothing less," came the General's response. "Now I will speak, and you will listen, for as I have said, I have limited time.

"You once spoke to me of a dream in which Wellington and I made peace over the dinner table. I thought you were a fool. But your dream stayed with me through my ill-fated Russian adventure as I watched my forces decimated by the cold, without provisions and harried on all sides by barbarians.

"I myself only barely managed to escape. With the help of the Polish and Lithuanian patriots I commandeered a sled and made for Paris, where my enemies were already celebrating my death.

"I raised a new army to fight in the name of France, but by then the whole of Europe was against me, and again I found my forces cornered and outnumbered. In perhaps the cruellest cut of all it was my old friend Monsieur de Metternich, who finally came to undermine me with an offer so insulting that I was forced to reject him. I had a notion to design a grand dinner meeting for my enemies, such as you had described in your dream; they with the forces of the sixth coalition at their back and I with what was left of my new Armée in support. But rather than a hearty meal, my idea was to serve them a poisoned chalice; to lull them into a false sense of security, while luring one or the other of them into a temporary alliance against the rest.

"When I did finally meet Wellington, it was not at the dinner table as you had dreamed. With my once great Armeé crumbling around me and my own allies in Paris turning against me, I was forced to make the greatest sacrifice of for the sake of my beloved France.

"My goose was well and truly cooked, as the English like to say."

Here he allows a wry smile to crease his lips.

"Nevertheless, here I am, wasting away like a dying man in this prison on a rock adrift in a godforsaken ocean, surrounded by buffoons."

Filipe, feeling curiously emboldened on the back of his previous outburst, retorts, "NO! You don't know what it is to waste away like a dying man. This place is luxury compared to the conditions your very own soldiers have been incarcerated and died in. You may call for cheese and wine on a whim. The only thing real prisoners may call out for is that God might have mercy on their souls.

"I have seen what happens in such places. Torture, deprivation, broken men."

Napoleon is not used to being lectured, "I fear that the years made you as bitter as they have me. This is not the tone I expected from the same man who once went to great pains to cook me a special meal."

"I am not a bitter man. I am a realistic man. I always admired you for your intellect, but your ambition turned into a great beast that threatened to devour you. I tried to sooth the beast within you in the only way I knew how - with my culinary skills, but as you ascended the heights of your own hubris you moved beyond the reach of any mere mortal."

Napoleon seems to regain some of the power that he lost. "My great reign was nothing short of history in the making. Books will be written about my exploits. What do you think the musings of cook will mean when weighed against my conquests? Do you really still believe that food can change the course of history?"

"I think high cuisine has the ability to appeal to our civilised natures, in just the same way that music is able to calm the soul."

"Too bad I am beyond reach, then, as you say."

"Yes. It's a shame… I shall leave here and return to my own happy little empire, where I have a wife, daughters, friends."

Filipe gets up off the chair and turns toward then door.

Napoleon reaches out and touches Filipe's arm, a gesture that would have been unthinkable during his reign.

A god would never touch a mere mortal. But the tables have turned now.

"Wait, where are you going?"

"I am going to do what I do best. I am going to cook for you."

He looks Napoleon in the eyes, "I am going to cook you your last supper."

The End

BON APPÉTIT

This book was created with the intention of spreading peace and joy among those who read it.

During our research for this book, we discovered that the idea of bringing good will through sharing a meal is a universal one across all cultures.

While this book contains true elements of history, it is Filipe's journey that informs the universe within it; his path is one of acceptance of the world around him simply as it is. There may be those on a different side or team, those of a different faith, or political bent, or those whose worldview is simply different from our own. Our message is that even in the face of disagreement, there is always a way forward.

So, call up a friend (or even one with whom you may have fallen out), and cook them something that comes from the heart. At the very least you will have the opportunity to learn a different perspective on something. Plus, there's nothing wrong with sharing a good meal.

Much love, the authors.